Who's to Know?

Books by Ann E. Weiss

Tune In, Tune Out: Broadcasting Regulation in
the United States

God and Government: The Separation of Church and State

The Nuclear Arms Race: Can We Survive It?

Good Neighbors? The United States and Latin America

Lies, Deception, and Truth

Who's to Know?

Information, the Media, and Public Awareness

Ann E. Weiss

Houghton Mifflin Company
Boston   1990

Library of Congress Cataloging-in-Publication Data

Weiss, Ann E., 1943–
 Who's to know? : information, the media, and public awareness /
Ann E. Weiss.
  p. cm.
 Includes bibliographical references.
 Summary: Does the public have a right to know? Discusses factors
that may interfere with that right and limit public knowledge, using
examples from current events which dramatize the complex issues of
media censorship.
 ISBN 0-395-49702-7
 1. Mass media—Censorship—Juvenile literature. 2. Freedom of
information—Juvenile literature. 3. Mass media—Objectivity—
Juvenile literature. 4. Privacy, Right of—Juvenile literature.
[1.Mass media—Censorship. 2. Freedom of information. 3. Privacy,
Right of.] I. Title.
P96.C64W4 1990   89-26901
363.2'.1—dc20   CIP
               AC

Printed in the United States of America

BP 10 9 8 7 6 5 4 3 2 1

To Rebecca

Contents

Who's to Know?

1

Late-Breaking News

News of the disaster broke on Friday, November 18, 1988. An earthquake had struck Yunnan Province in the southern part of the People's Republic of China. Ten thousand men, women, and children were dead.

And another item of interest: the quake had occurred in 1970 — *eighteen years* before Chinese authorities permitted word of it to be made public.

When exactly in 1970? The authorities weren't saying. Where precisely in Yunnan Province? No word on that, either. Officials at China's State Seismology Bureau were willing to add only that the quake had been centered under a town. That, they said, explained the high death toll.

Why the reluctance to part with information? Why the eighteen-year veil of secrecy? No one outside the top ranks of China's ruling Communist party could say for sure. All anyone knew was that since 1949, the year the People's Republic was formed and communism became the way of life in China, Chinese leaders have been among the world's most secretive. They have routinely tried to downplay — or altogether suppress — news about such events as earthquakes, airplane crashes, and industrial accidents. Only if citizens of other countries chanced to be killed or injured in a particular disaster were many details revealed.

China's leaders have been reticent on other matters as well. They have refused to talk about economic problems, for example, or about reports of corrupt officials. For nearly forty years the government declined to publish its own laws! Even tax laws, including those that applied to foreign businesses, were often kept secret. Not until the late 1980s did the leadership begin publicizing legal codes and relaxing its strict stand against providing information. By the spring of 1989 the relaxation had extended to allowing reporters and camera crews from America's Cable News Network (CNN) to record an uprising by Chinese students and workers demanding democratic reforms. As we will see in more detail later, the uprising was to end in violence and a government clampdown on information leaving the country.

Chinese leaders were hardly unique in their secrecy. Until the mid-1980s, and the beginning of other changes, it was difficult to get much detailed information about what was going on in the Soviet Union, China's neighbor to the west. The Soviet Union's communist leaders inherited a long tradition of secrecy and government control of information from the czars and princes who had ruled Russia for centuries. Facts about the country's economy, industries, crop failures, labor problems, food

shortages, and social, religious, and political dissent —
all were in as short supply after the Soviets seized power
in 1917 as they had been before. Until the end of the
1980s it was much the same in such Eastern European
nations as Poland, Hungary, and East Germany.

Communist nations are not the only ones in which
information control is the rule. Many right-wing governments, like that of ultraconservative South Africa, also
decide what is to be published and broadcast inside the
country and to the outside world.

South Africa is a nation of about thirty-three million
people. Just under six million are white. From these six
million come South Africa's rulers, its professionals and
civil servants, its business leaders and high-salaried
workers. For them, life means modern, comfortable
homes in attractive neighborhoods; good schools and col-
leges; the liberty to come and go as they please; the right
to vote in national elections.

For the other twenty-seven million South Africans, the
majority of whom are black, things are different. Most
live herded together in special "townships," where
houses are shacklike, schools overcrowded and poorly
equipped, and medical care almost nonexistent. Black
men frequently live apart from their families in work
camps located near the mines and factories where they
spend long hours at dangerous jobs in return for subsis-
tence wages. Blacks may vote only in local township
elections. The South African policy of strict segregation
of the races is called apartheid.

Over the years, antiapartheid feelings on the part of blacks — and some whites — have led to protests. In 1986 the growing violence prompted the government to declare a state of emergency. Under it, protesters could be imprisoned without trial for months or years at a time. Antiapartheid groups could be outlawed. The news media could be silenced.

Silencing the media was a must, South African leaders thought. Preventing the press from reporting on the violence would not stop it, but would keep it out of the public eye. Out of sight, out of mind for the protesters — or so South Africa's white rulers hoped. Eventually, deprived of an international audience, and international sympathy, the antiapartheid movement would lose influence. South African leaders, like those who govern in the Soviet Union, the People's Republic of China, and Eastern Europe, have assumed the right to control public awareness according to their own needs and wishes.

Leaders in a great many other countries assume the same right. Raymond D. Gastil of New York City's Freedom House, a conservative research foundation, found that in the 1980s a majority of governments worldwide were practicing press censorship. The governments of three quarters of the world's nations, Gastil reported, "have a significant or dominant voice in determining what does or does not appear in the media."

The U.S. government is not one of them. By anyone's standard the United States must be counted among that fortunate 25 percent of nations in which people have every right and opportunity to know what is going on at home and abroad. And yet . . .

News of the disaster broke on Friday, October 14, 1988. Thousands of tons of radioactive uranium wastes had been released into the air and water in Fernald, Ohio, a few miles west of Cincinnati. The wastes had come from a U.S.-government-owned plant where uranium is enriched for use in nuclear weapons. Although plant operators and federal officials knew of the contamination, they had kept quiet about it. Keeping quiet meant not cleaning it up, since any cleanup would have involved publicity. Thousands of local residents had been exposed to the radiation, which has been proven to cause cancer.

And another item of interest: the exposure had started in 1951 — *thirty-seven years* before U.S. authorities permitted word of it to be made public.

Why? Don't Americans have a right to know about radiation in the air they breathe and the water they drink? Don't they have a right to information about safety conditions in installations built and operated at taxpayers' expense? Isn't there, in the United States of all places, a public right to know?

2

Old and New World Censorship

Certainly there is a right to know in the United States. There has to be, since the United States is a democracy. No country can sustain a democratic government without a well-informed citizenry.

America's Founding Fathers knew that. As Thomas Jefferson, author of the Declaration of Independence and the nation's third president, put it, "A democracy cannot be both ignorant and free." James Madison, who helped draw up the U.S. Constitution and succeeded Jefferson as president, agreed. "Knowledge will forever govern ignorance," he wrote, "and a people who mean to be their own Governors, must arm themselves with the power which knowledge brings."

If the citizens of the new United States neglected to arm themselves thus, Madison and Jefferson warned, they would be little better off than they had been as subjects of the British crown. True, they would have their national independence, but unless Americans took care to share information fully among themselves, knowledge — and power — would be concentrated in the hands of a privileged few. The states would face the threat of tyranny in the future as surely as the colonies had endured its reality in the past. For it was a tradition of tyranny and official control of information, not one of democracy and openness, that the New World settlers had brought with them from their Old World homelands.

The tradition of tyranny had ancient roots. There probably never was a time when human beings lacked the means or the will to try to control what their fellow creatures might think and know. Even in prehistoric days, before people could read or write, some limits must have been set upon the spoken word. How else could one clan or family have kept secret its special knowledge — rituals and healing spells, favorite hunting places, plans for dealing with clan rivalries, and the like?

After writing was invented in Mesopotamia over 5,000 years ago, censorship needs changed. Written information could be passed on more efficiently and in a more permanent form than before. And a family's or a village's secrets were at greater risk. Leaders, religious and secular, must have had to take new steps to make sure secrets did not fall into unfriendly hands.

The years passed and civilization evolved. Villages became towns, and then cities. Tribal leadership turned into organized government with organized politics. War was no longer a matter of local skirmishes but of thought-out invasions and long campaigns. The need for secrecy grew. After the powerful city-state of Rome extended its empire over most of Europe about 2,000 years ago, its rulers found themselves issuing censorship decrees from Armenia and the Arabian desert in the east to England and the Scottish border in the west.

Rome's empire fell late in the fifth century A.D., overrun by Huns, Visigoths, and other warlike peoples from central and eastern Europe. Over the next centuries government was weak and decentralized, and secular censorship was largely a matter of local enforcement. Religious censorship, however, was becoming widespread and rigorous.

Throughout the Middle Ages, which lasted from about 800 to around the end of the fourteenth century, the Roman Catholic church was Europe's foremost censor. The church's concern was primarily in protecting Catholics from the sin of heresy — believing in something that went against accepted doctrine. Church leaders therefore adopted strict measures aimed at keeping people from seeing or hearing anything that contradicted official teachings. But their censorship spilled over into secular areas as well, since church and state acted, theoretically at least, as one. Church leaders backed the information-control efforts of kings and local princes, who in turn helped enforce religious censorship.

The censorship of the Middle Ages, both secular and religious, was primarily of the type that is called punitive. That is, offenders were punished after the fact for writing anything the authorities considered dangerous. Common punishments were imprisonment or exile.

By the early 1500s the Middle Ages were well past,

and the new century saw the introduction in Europe of the other broad form of censorship — prior restraint. Prior restraint, or preventive censorship, requires people to get official permission ahead of time to write or publish. The authorities turned to prior restraint in response to Johann Gutenberg's invention, several decades earlier, of the printing press. Gutenberg is believed to have built Europe's first press in Mainz, Germany, sometime in the 1430s.

The technology of printing changed civilization — and civilization's methods for controlling information — just as the invention of writing had changed them millennia before. Before printing, books and other documents existed only in handwritten form. Each manuscript — the word comes from the Latin *manu*, "hand," and *scriptus*, "writing" — had to be copied individually, with slow and painstaking care. Manuscripts were so rare and expensive that only the rich and powerful had access to them or to the information they contained. Ordinary folk, entirely lacking written matter, remained dependent for information on gossip, hearsay, and rumor.

The printing press took information out of the exclusive possession of the few and made it available to the many. As more and more presses went into operation, the written word evolved from a rarity into something nearly commonplace. By the late 1400s street venders were peddling "broadsides," large single sheets printed on just one side. With their spirited accounts of royal scandals, natural disasters, and reported miracles, broadsides were

remote ancestors of our modern newspapers. Other ancestors were pamphlets containing information about recent events at home and abroad. Although these early
pamphlets were more serious and substantial than broadsides, they were hardly more reliable as sources of ob-
jective information. Most were highly partisan, written
by people with definite opinions on the important issues
of the day.

Those issues were controversial. Some involved political matters, such as national or international disputes and
alliances. Others were religious. The sixteenth century
saw the beginnings of Europe's Protestant Reformation
and the religious rivalries sparked by that movement.
Often religious and political issues were linked. England's King Henry VIII, for instance, broke with the
Roman Catholic church in the 1530s after the pope refused him permission to divorce his first wife, Catherine
of Aragon. One reason for the refusal: the pope was a
political ally of Catherine's powerful nephew, the king of
Spain.

Pamphleteers on every side, Catholic and Protestant,
pro-England and pro-Spain, for Henry and against him,
would have had a fine time debating the ins and outs of
the matter in public, except for one thing. The authorities
wouldn't let them. Already those authorities could sense
that people were finding the printed word far more convincing than hearsay. Along with the power to print went
the power to inform and persuade, and the authorities
rightly saw that power as a challenge to their own abso-

lute sovereignty. They did not hesitate to act accordingly.

Pope Alexander VI was among the first to issue a prior restraint decree. In 1501 Alexander announced that from then on, church authorities would examine all writings before giving permission for them to appear in print. Only those books and articles that fully supported official church doctrine would be approved for publication. Sixty years later another pope, Pius VI, invoked a different form of prior restraint by commissioning an Index of Prohibited Books. Most of the works on the list had been judged to be heretical, and anyone who read one faced the punishment devout Catholics dreaded above all others: excommunication. Excommunication meant not being allowed to take the holy sacraments and thereby being denied all hope of heaven after death. Protestant leaders like John Knox in Scotland and John Calvin in France imposed rigid censorship rules of their own in towns and regions where Protestantism was the officially established faith.

Secular leaders similarly depended upon prior restraint to silence controversy. In 1534 England's Henry VIII ordered all printers to obtain government licenses before setting up shop. The rule allowed the authorities to muzzle anyone whose views they considered socially, religiously, or politically unsound. Four years later Henry issued a list of forbidden books. Over the next two centuries Europe's other absolute monarchs, equally determined to repress debate and dissent, followed his example of censorship. Together, church and state continued to maintain tight control over the flow of information in Europe.

And in America. When Europeans began colonizing North America in the 1600s, they brought with them their heritage of religious intolerance enforced by secular authority and secular rules backed by religious leaders. They brought with them also the European enthusiasm for censorship. The rules were especially strict in such Massachusetts settlements as Salem and Boston. When in 1635 a Salem minister named Roger Williams entered into a religious dispute with other local clergymen, he was banished by authority of the Massachusetts General Court. The next year Williams founded Providence, in Rhode Island, and invited people of all religious faiths to join him there. Open discussion was welcome in Providence.

But that colony was unusual, and religious and political repression remained the rule elsewhere. In New Amsterdam, on what is now the lower end of New York City's Manhattan Island, Governor Peter Stuyvesant enforced Holland's particular brand of Protestantism. After the English gained control of the area, the Church of England became the established religion. Virginia, too, was Church of England. Pennsylvania, home to members of the Society of Friends, or Quakers, was more liberal. Non-Christians were permitted to live there, although they could not vote or hold public office.

Colonial leaders also copied European rulers in maintaining political secrecy. During the 1600s printing was licensed in America as strictly as in England. The first New World printer — a Virginia man with the interesting name of William Nuthead — opened for business in 1682 but was forbidden to print a word about the deliberations of the colony's lawmaking body, its House of Burgesses. The first American newspaper, *Publick Occurrences,* appeared in Boston on September 25, 1690. Its promise — "Furnished Once a Moneth or if any Glut of Occurrences happen, oftener" — was not to be fulfilled. The premier edition contained news of local politics and criticized colonial authorities for certain of their dealings with the Native Americans. Outraged, the authorities shut the paper down for good.

Censorship rules were also tight in Pennsylvania, where founder William Penn presided over a council meeting at which it was decided not to publish the colony's laws. Communist China is apparently not the only place where legal codes have deliberately been kept secret. Pennsylvania was also the site of the first American criminal trial on what we would call a right-to-know issue. Colonial leaders brought a charge of seditious libel against printer William Bradford. Seditious libel was defined as the publishing of something that was likely to incite public protest. The "something" in this case was a copy of the colony's royal charter. Convicted, the printer served over a year in jail.

Gradually the controls were loosened. In 1735 a New York printer named John Peter Zenger was, like Bradford, hauled into court on a libel charge. He had published criticism of the colony's governor in his newspaper, the *Weekly Journal*. Unlike Bradford, Zenger was acquitted after his lawyer pointed out that what Zenger had printed was no more than the simple truth. The truth cannot be a libel, the lawyer argued, and the court agreed. The verdict flew in the face of English law, which held that truth was *not* a defense against a libel charge — and held further that "the greater the truth, the greater the libel." The Zenger verdict marked an important step along the road to establishing the American right to know.

There were others. In 1747 the New York Assembly announced that henceforth its proceedings could be reported. In 1776 the Massachusetts General Court, which 141 years earlier had sent Roger Williams into exile, opened its doors to the public. In making themselves available to the scrutiny of the people, America's colonial institutions were again imitating institutions in the mother country. In 1771 Parliament had renounced its long-standing practice of keeping debates strictly secret, and English prepublication licensing laws had been eased starting in 1695. On the eve of the American Revolution, then, people on both sides of the Atlantic were moving away from the censorship and tyranny of former times.

The colonists won their revolution in 1783. For four years after that the new United States drifted along with little in the way of central government or authority. Quarrels broke out among the states, and the country seemed on the verge of falling apart. At last, in February 1787,

Congress officially called for setting up a federal government strong enough to compel the states to act as one nation. On May 14 delegates from twelve of the thirteen states met in Philadelphia to write a constitution defining that government and ordering its workings. Only Rhode Island chose not to be represented at the Constitutional Convention.

The men assembled in Philadelphia decided that if they kept their work secret, it would go faster. They may have been right. Their deliberations were conducted in private, and by September 17 the Constitution was ready to be presented to the state legislatures for ratification. As soon as nine of the thirteen voted to accept the document, it would become binding upon the nation.

But ratification did not come immediately — in part because of the silence that had surrounded the convention. That silence worried Americans still in the process of shaking off the secrecy and authoritarianism of the past. Just exactly what degree of federalism did this Constitution call for, anyway? they wondered. Were individual liberties adequately protected? Legislators in a number of states said they would agree to ratify, but only if Congress promised to amend the Constitution to spell out citizens' rights — freedom of religion, speech, and the press; the right to carry firearms; and so on. Congress agreed to do so, and on June 21, 1788, New Hampshire became the ninth state to ratify. The Constitution went into effect on March 4 of the next year. Just over three months later Congress enacted the Bill of Rights. It, too, received state ratification and officially took effect on December 15, 1791.

The future looked bright to Americans that day. They had their independence, a Constitution, and the individual rights they had sought. (That is, free white males had those rights. Women, Native Americans, slaves, and black freedmen would have to wait a long time to enjoy them.) Not even white men, however, had the right to know, nor would they for years to come.

3

What Right to Know?

It may sound peculiar to say that the Americans of 1791 lacked the right to know since they did have the First Amendment assurance of freedom of speech and the press. But though the right to free speech is *part* of the right to know, it is not *all* of it. The right to know goes beyond freedom from censorship. It consists, according to James Russell Wiggins, former editor of the *Washington Post*, of five separate rights.

Two of these rights have to do directly with free speech: freedom from prior restraint and freedom from punitive censorship. The other elements of the right to know, says Wiggins, are the right to collect information; the right to have access to the media and materials essential for communicating that information; and the right to distribute the information — to make it directly available to individual members of the public — without interference from government under the law or from private groups acting outside the law.

The Americans of 1791 had no particular claim to any right to gather, communicate, or disseminate informa-

tion. Even their right to freedom from prior restraint and punitive censorship was soon thrown into jeopardy. The Bill of Rights was not yet seven years old when Congress enacted, and President John Adams signed into law, a censorship measure.

The Sedition Act of 1798 gave federal authorities the right to prosecute anyone suspected of plotting against the federal government. Reasonable enough. However, one section of the law also made it a crime to speak or write of the president or Congress "with the intent to defame" or to bring either "into contempt or disrepute." The provision made it possible for those in power to charge with sedition not only dangerous conspirators, but *anyone* who criticized them. It made the Sedition Act a potential tool for stifling legitimate political discussion.

And that was exactly how the act was used. First to be convicted under the law was Matthew Lyon, a U.S. congressman from Vermont. Lyon had criticized President Adams in a Vermont newspaper, saying he had "a continual grasp for power" and "an unbounded thirst for ridiculous pomp, foolish adulation and selfish avarice." He also quoted from a letter sent by an American then living in France to the effect that Congress ought to send Adams to the madhouse. Lyon was fined $1,000 and sentenced to four months in prison. Reelected while behind bars, he was one of ten jailed under the Sedition Act. The act expired in 1800 and was not renewed. So ended one threat to Americans' freedom of speech.

Other threats followed, but by no means all originated

at the federal level. Many came from the states. Indeed, by the middle of the nineteenth century, nearly half of the states had placed limits on freedom of the press. The issue that provoked the censorship was slavery.

In the 1600s slavery had been practiced in every colony, but two centuries later it remained legal only in the southern United States. During the first half of the 1800s some Americans began campaigning to abolish it everywhere. Abolitionist sentiment, particularly strong in the North, was met by resistance from the South and a determination to cling to what people there considered an essential institution. By the time the Civil War broke out between North and South in 1861, every Southern state but Kentucky had outlawed the publication of abolitionist materials.

How could the states get away with defying the First Amendment? The answer lies in the amendment itself. Its wording is unlike that of the rest of the Bill of Rights. In the Second through the Tenth amendments, the rights of the people are expressed in an absolute way: this action may not be taken against them, or they are to enjoy that freedom. The First Amendment is different. "Congress," it says, "shall make no law . . . abridging the freedom of speech, or of the press." The key word is the first one, "Congress." The amendment limited what Congress could do, but failed to place the same restriction on lawmaking bodies at lower levels of government. So state legislators could claim rights, including the right to censor, that federal lawmakers could not.

The situation changed after the North won the Civil War in 1865 and the reunited nation ratified the Fourteenth Amendment. That amendment says, "No State shall make or enforce any law which shall abridge the privileges . . . of citizens of the United States; nor shall any State deprive any person of life, liberty, or property, without due process of law." The words make the First Amendment binding upon government below the federal level.

Other limitations on Americans' free-speech rights have come in times of national crisis. During the Civil War, President Abraham Lincoln empowered federal agents to open and censor mail. He also authorized the shutting down of newspapers that expressed anti-Union points of view, and he ordered one paper, the *Washington Sunday Chronicle,* seized for revealing the movements of Union troops.

How could the chief executive of a democracy indulge in such unconstitutional actions? How could he not? Lincoln might have retorted. Sometimes the end must justify the means. It was wartime and the country was fighting for its very life. What would be the point of permitting anti-Union dissent, which would create more division, and perhaps undermine the North's military effort, enable the South to win the war, and thereby destroy the United States? Preserving constitutional rights was important in Lincoln's eyes, but preserving the Constitution itself was more so. "Are all the laws but one to go unexecuted, and government itself go to pieces, lest that one be violated?" the president demanded.

Other presidents have asked the same question in different words. Generally their answers have been, like Lincoln's, No. Wartime censorship is common in this country, as in every other, and in this century, too. Federal, state, and local censors were busy, for example, during both World War I and World War II.

In each conflict this country fought with England, France, Russia, and other nations against Germany and its allies. In the course of World War I (1914–1918; the United States joined the fighting in 1917), Congress authorized a federal Censorship Board. The board took mailing privileges away from newspapers it considered anti-American and banned at least one magazine outright. "Subversive" books were cleared off library shelves.

The World War I years also saw the passage by Congress of the Espionage Act of 1917 and the Sedition Act of 1918. The former made it a crime to say or write anything that might encourage disloyalty or interfere with the drafting of men to serve in the army. The latter made it a crime to utter "disloyal or abusive language" about the government, the Constitution, the flag — even the military uniform. Over 1,500 men and women were arrested and charged under the acts. During World War II (1939–1945; American involvement began in 1941) it was illegal to advocate the violent overthrow of government at any level or to do, say, or write anything that might encourage disloyalty or insubordination in the military.

After World War II ended, U.S. censors took aim at

another target: communism. (Communists had been subjected to censorship during the two world wars as well.) Although the fighting was over, millions of Americans regarded the nation as still at risk. They were obsessed with the idea that unknown numbers of agents of the Soviet Union, many of them traitorous American citizens, had infiltrated the government, labor unions, schools and universities, and most of all, the mass media of radio, television, and motion pictures. Now, they were convinced, those agents were preparing to betray their country to Russia. Members of Congress were as certain as anyone else that the danger was real, and in 1950 they enacted a law that required all members of the Communist party to register with the U.S. Attorney General, kept communists from other countries from entering the United States, forbade alien communists already in America to acquire passports or work in defense plants, and gave the president the authority to jail those aliens in the event of war.

Over the following years, this and other laws were used, as the Sedition Act of 1798 had been, more to quell dissent than to protect the nation against genuine conspirators. Hundreds of men and women, nearly all of them completely loyal Americans, were brought before Congress and questioned as to their political views. Once more, publications that merely hinted at criticism of the United States, or at support for what were thought to be left-wing ideas, disappeared from libraries. Even stories about Robin Hood — that legendary embodiment of the "communistic" idea that it is right to take from the rich and give to the poor — were banned in some places.

Yet even in the midst of the persecution, censorship, and political intolerance of the 1950s, the concept of a right to know was slowly making itself felt in American life.

One signal of the emergence of this concept came from the U.S. Supreme Court, the nation's highest court of law. Back in 1919 the court had reviewed the case of *Schenck v. U.S.* (The *v.* stands for *versus,* "against" in Latin.) Charles T. Schenck, convicted of being a draft resister under the World War I Espionage Act appealed his conviction to the court, arguing that the act violated his First Amendment rights. The court disagreed and upheld the conviction. But the justices made it clear that they had done so only because Schenck had written an antidraft pamphlet in wartime, when raising an army could be considered essential to the national security. If he had written the pamphlet in a time of peace, the decision might have been different. "The question in every case," the high court explained, "is whether the words used . . . create a clear and present danger."

"A clear and present danger." The words became a yardstick by which the censorship rights of government — as opposed to the free-speech rights of individuals — came to be measured in this country. In Schenck's case the justices thought the danger real. But as the years went by, they began using the clear-and-present-danger standard to grant the American people ever-wider latitude to criticize and condemn.

In the mid-1940s the court also extended Americans'

"right to receive" information. The case involved a religious group, the Jehovah's Witnesses.

Jehovah's Witnesses actively proselytize for their faith, visiting people door to door to spread their religious message. Many outside the sect find the visits annoying, and a number of towns and cities had reacted to citizens' complaints by passing laws forbidding neighborhood solicitations. Were such local ordinances legal? No, said the Supreme Court. Americans have a right to be exposed to new ideas. Two years later it went further, upholding workers' "right to hear" a speech by a labor union organizer. However, it was not until 1965 that the court spoke in so many words of the "right to know." In the case of *Griswold v. Connecticut* the justices ruled that a state could not make it illegal to offer birth control information to adults.

Four years after that, the court extended the right to know to all areas of public life. The extension came in a case involving the broadcasting industry's so-called fairness doctrine. That doctrine was imposed on the industry in the 1930s by the Federal Communications Commission (FCC), which regulates radio and television. It required station owners who broadcast editorial opinions on a controversial issue to offer time on the air to people with other opinions on the same issue. The policy was unpopular with broadcasters, and in the 1969 case they argued against it on the grounds that it violated their First Amendment rights. The federal government didn't presume to tell newspaper publishers how they must and must not inform readers, station owners said. It ought to be the same in broadcasting.

The FCC disagreed. Publishing and broadcasting are different, the commissioners asserted. Anyone with a typewriter and a copier (today it would be a word processor and a facsimile — fax — machine) can bring his or her opinions to public attention in a newspaper or newsletter of sorts. But the airwaves are a limited resource. They belong to the public, but only so many frequencies are available for broadcasting. And setting up a station of one's own is not as simple or as cheap as putting out a newsletter. The right of public access to the airwaves had to be protected, FCC lawyers told the justices. The justices concurred, upholding the fairness doctrine. It is "crucial," the court concluded, for ". . . the public to receive suitable access to social, political, esthetic, moral, and other ideas and experiences."

Not only did Americans now have the right to get information over the airwaves and in their own homes, they were about to have it in a growing list of public places. The right to receive and distribute information — even controversial information — in such public areas as streets and parks is traditional in this country. Late in the 1960s the courts added public facilities like bus and train stations to the places where information may be received and disseminated. Even in a privately owned shopping mall protest literature may be handed out, as long as the protest is in some way related to regular mall activity.

At the same time that the courts were making Americans' right to know a matter of legal precedent, Congress was making it a matter of legislation. In 1966 lawmakers passed the Freedom of Information Act (FOIA). That law opened up the executive branch of government to citizens, giving them the right to obtain information from all the federal agencies that operate under the direction of the president.

"In principle," says John Anthony Scott, professor of law at Rutgers University in New Jersey, the FOIA "opened up the entire vast body of documentation in the keeping of the federal authorities to the scrutiny of the public." Before the law went into effect in July 1967, anyone who wanted information from the executive branch had to prove he or she needed that information — that it was necessary in order to prepare a defense in a court case, for instance. Now all anyone had to do to get information was to put in a formal written request. "Need" had changed to "right."

Who has used the FOIA and for what? People living near a nuclear power station in Kentucky used it to find out about flaws in the plant's construction — and to shut the plant down. Women have called on the FOIA to get the facts about sex discrimination in the workplace. Labor union members have invoked it to learn about job-related health and safety hazards. Close to 100,000 individuals whose names appear in the files of the Central Intelligence Agency (CIA) and the Federal Bureau of Investigation (FBI) have turned to the FOIA to find out what information has been collected about them. News reporters have used the FOIA, too. They used it extensively, for instance, in the 1970s in the course of investigating what came to be known as the Watergate affair.

The Watergate is a hotel-office-apartment complex in Washington, D.C. During the 1972 presidential election campaign, members of the Democratic political party rented offices there. In the early morning hours of June 17, those offices were broken into. The seven men arrested in connection with the break-in were charged with going through the Democrats' files, stealing some documents and photographing others.

What had the burglars been after? The obvious assumption was that they had been looking for Democratic secrets and strategies, hoping to get information that Republicans could use against their opponents in the fall campaign. But had the spies been acting with the approval of Republican leaders? Had Republican President Richard M. Nixon, who was planning to run for reelection in the fall, known what was going on? Nixon denied all criminal knowledge, and so did other top Republicans. Most Americans believed them. In November the voters gave the president a landslide victory.

But even as Nixon began his second term of office, his presidency was crumbling. Reporters and others looking into the Watergate break-in discovered that the burglars had indeed been in the pay of the Republican party. Acting under the FOIA, the investigators requested information from executive branch agencies, and they got it. Over the months the investigation moved closer and closer to the White House. Eventually it reached the president's Oval Office, and on August 5, 1974, Nixon admitted that he had known about the Watergate burglary from the beginning. Within a week of its happening, he had ordered the FBI to halt its investigation into the affair. Four days after making that admission, Nixon resigned, the only U.S. president ever forced to do so.

Watergate left most Americans convinced of the value of the FOIA and other right-to-know rules and precedents. Without them the truth about the scandal might never have been discovered. Shortly after Nixon left office, Congress voted to strengthen some of the FOIA's original provisions to make it even easier and quicker to get information from the executive branch. Freedom of information laws were enacted at lower levels of government as well. By the end of the 1970s the future of Americans' right to know seemed assured.

Was it? In 1981 Ronald W. Reagan took the oath of office as the fortieth president of the United States. The nation's new leader was committed to the belief that government and its agencies work best when they are free of interference from "uninformed" laymen. Just nine days after entering the White House, Reagan announced that he was canceling two new federal rules that were about to take effect. The first would have broadened the right of patients in nursing homes to examine their own records. The second would have required the National Highway Traffic Safety Administration to tell car buyers how well their vehicles had performed in crash tests.

As time passed, the Reagan administration took additional steps aimed at increasing secrecy in government. The CIA was ordered to abolish its Office of Public Affairs, reducing reporters' access to information about the agency's activities. The libraries maintained by various federal agencies, which had been open to the public, were converted to government use only. Reagan also encouraged the FCC to scrap its fairness doctrine, and in 1987 it did. The commissioners agreed that there were so many more radio and television stations in the 1980s than there had been in the 1930s, when the rule was instituted, or even in 1969, when it was endorsed by the Supreme Court, that the doctrine was no longer needed. In 1985 and 1986 Reagan succeeded in getting Congress to alter the FOIA, making it more expensive and more cumbersome for people to obtain information from the executive branch. We will look at these alterations, and at other Reagan-era information restrictions, more closely in Chapter Nine.

The new administration was tight-lipped in other ways. Reagan rarely talked with reporters, and officials who conducted press briefings at the various executive departments grew steadily less communicative. According to journalist Eve Pell, the spokesperson at one State Department session responded to reporters' questions with "No comment," "Can't say," "Don't know," or "I have nothing for you on that" thirty times in a single forty-five-minute period.

Pell sees an ominous pattern in all this. So do others

who believe that the right to know is essential in any democracy. After three hundred years of moving in the direction of an increasingly informed society, they believe, that movement has stopped, reversed itself. They fear the United States may be headed toward a new era of official secrecy.

Others dismiss the notion, scoffing at the idea that the federal government would try to force a return to the secretiveness and censorship of the past. Even if it did try, they add, it wouldn't succeed with the country's present information and communications media in place. Those media are numerous enough — and varied, rich, independent, and powerful enough — to provide a bulwark capable of preserving Americans' right to know.

4

The Media —
Keys to an Informed Society?

Our modern sources of information bear little resemblance to those of years gone by, when news was a rare commodity. During the first eight decades of settlement in the New World not a single newspaper was printed anywhere in the colonies. When one finally did appear, it was promptly suppressed by the authorities.

Today newspapers abound. According to the *World Almanac,* 1,645 daily papers were being published in the United States in 1987. Nearly 63 million copies are sold each day. The country's 820 Sunday papers sell a total of about 63 million each week. Besides daily and Sunday newspapers, Americans can choose from "alternative" weeklies like the *Boston Phoenix,* the *Miami New Times,* and San Francisco's *Bay Guardian.* The Association of Alternative Newsweeklies estimates that its 55 member papers enjoy a combined readership of 5 to 6 million. At that, the association represents only about a third of the country's weekly offerings.

Other forms of printed matter, scarce in colonial America, are readily available to us. Magazines were unheard of until the mid-1600s and uncommon for most of a century after that. In its 1989 list of leading U.S. magazines the *World Almanac* included the names of 184 periodicals. Circulations ranged from a high of almost 17 million to a low of just over 300,000. Books, too, are far more numerous now than formerly. Figures collected by the trade journal *Publishers Weekly* indicate that 45,401 titles made it into print in the United States in 1987.

The print media may have been limited in the past, but the nonprint media didn't exist at all until about the last century and a half. Photography came along in the mid-1800s, and motion pictures followed around 1900. These two new forms revolutionized communication much the way the invention of the printing press had four hundred years earlier. Just as people back then found printed matter more persuasive than speech, so men and women one hundred years ago discovered that news photos and films make words more convincing and that seeing truly is believing.

Radio was also new at the start of the twentieth century. Now radios are everywhere — in automobiles, as headphones, built into novelty items, even in stuffed animals. Television did not become a fixture of American life until after World War II. Today over 90 million U.S. households — 98 percent of the total — have at least one television set. More than 53 million households have two or more. Commercial television stations numbered 1,017 in 1988, and noncommercial, or public educational, stations, 325. Forty-two million families have access to cable television, and almost half of all television homes receive between nine and fourteen different channels. Television started out as an entertainment medium, as did radio and motion pictures. So, in a sense, did newspapers, which after all evolved in part from the titillating broadsides of the late 1400s. But movies, radio, and TV, like newspapers, soon came to serve an informational function as well. Movie theater managers began showing a newsreel along with the feature film. And of course features themselves can be informational in nature. The 1976 Academy Award–winning *All the President's Men,* for instance, told the true story of the unraveling of the Watergate affair. Radio took on an informational role when early station operators began interrupting their musical offerings (music has always been a staple of radio) to read newspaper headlines or dispense practical advice. In 1920 a Pittsburgh station, KDKA, made its debut with minute-by-minute reports of the returns of that year's presidential election. The broadcast marked the start of an election-night tradition that has grown steadily more elaborate. By the 1950s television was bringing the "seeing is believing" impact of movie house newsreels into the nation's living rooms with a nightly fifteen minutes of news. In the 1960s the broadcasts were lengthened to a half hour.

Half an hour, less the eight minutes normally set aside for advertising. A "half-hour" newscast contains just twenty-two minutes of information on the country's three major commercial networks — the American Broadcasting Company (ABC), the Columbia Broadcasting System (CBS), and the National Broadcasting Company (NBC). Is twenty-two minutes enough time to give viewers a thorough understanding of the day's events?

Many think not. Sure, it's time enough to say that an airplane has made an emergency landing in Iowa, that the president left at noon for a weekend vacation, that Congress is debating a new weapons system, and that scientists at an international convention have issued a warning about the link between air pollution and a possible global warming trend. Viewers will see dramatic footage of the emergency landing and watch as the president waves goodbye and boards his helicopter. They'll listen as a reporter at the U.S. Capitol tells them what a few members of Congress think of the new weapon. Satellite transmission will enable scientists in different parts of the world to exchange a few words about climate and pollution.

But the exchange won't teach viewers much about the link between pollution and climate. A few words are not sufficient to explain such a complex subject — or so many people claim. "Television is not an adequate medium to . . . inform the public on complicated issues," says Walter Cronkite, himself a former CBS anchorman. "The half-hour news broadcast is not the medium for this sort of thing." The problem, as Cronkite and others see it, is not just that twenty-two minutes is too short a time to explain complicated issues, but that television is an overwhelmingly visual medium. What viewers become informed about may have more to do with the subject's pictorial qualities and dramatic impact than with its real significance. Footage of a plane's emergency landing may be given airtime at the expense of details about Congress's objections to a new weapons system, for instance. What the evening news amounts to, many critics contend, is a headline service. Climatic threat and presidential holiday, emergency landing and billion-dollar weapons system — all get jumbled up together and come out sounding equally important, or unimportant, when the news is over and the viewer goes back to game shows or sitcom reruns.

Still, there's more to informational television than network evening newscasts. The networks run morning news programs as well, and late-night talk shows. They air Sunday talk shows too, and "This Week with David Brinkley," "Face the Nation," and "Meet the Press" give press correspondents an opportunity to meet with newsmakers and discuss issues in some detail. Even on such shows, though, says writer and media critic Gore Vidal, no interview is allowed to run more than seven minutes without commercial interruption, and three minutes is more common.

On rare occasions, however, the networks suspend regular programming for continuous coverage of a breaking story such as a space shuttle takeoff or landing. There are also news "magazine" programs like "60 Minutes" and "20/20," and "docudramas"— fictionalized retellings of events that really happened. Other choices open to viewers include such lively and popular talk shows as

"Donahue," with host Phil Donahue, "The Oprah Winfrey Show," and "Geraldo," with the flamboyant Geraldo Rivera, a former network journalist.

There are also television news sources beyond ABC, CBS, and NBC. The noncommercial Public Broadcasting System (PBS) broadcasts "Washington Week in Review" on Friday nights, and PBS viewers can tune in daily to "The MacNeil-Lehrer Newshour." The latter is television's only five-day-a-week, hour-long news program and, thanks to PBS's no-ads policy, it actually does take up nearly the full hour.

Viewers with cable have other options. Subscribers can get an all-weather channel, an all-financial one, and one devoted to consumer affairs. C-Span carries major congressional debates and committee hearings in full. Cable News Network was established in 1980 as a twenty-four-hour headline service, with periodic but superficial updates of breaking stories from around the globe. In the spring of 1989, however, the network "came of age," according to Fred Friendly, formerly of CBS and now professor emeritus at the Columbia University Graduate School of Journalism. Friendly was referring to CNN's coverage of events in the People's Republic of China.

Those events began in early May when Chinese students confronted their communist leaders with demands for freedom of the press and a more democratic political system. The students, tens of thousands of them, gathered at Tiananmen Square, in the heart of Beijing, China's capital. There they stayed for weeks, setting up camps and staging orderly and peaceful demonstrations. As time passed, the students were joined by people from all walks of life. Eventually, as many as a million men, women, and children were packed into the square. Broadcasting via satellite, Cable News provided up to thirty hours per week of live reporting from the scene, far more than any of the three major networks had time to provide. Extensive interviews with students, civilians, and government officials allowed viewers to see and hear exactly what was going on.

Even President George Bush tuned in. Why, reporters asked White House aides, would the president rely on CNN for information when he had the CIA and all the other agencies of government to turn to? According to Maureen Dowd of the *New York Times,* the network actually "had more people and more sophisticated equipment on the scene than United States diplomatic and intelligence outposts did."

In the end, though, CNN coverage failed. Late in May the government ordered army units to converge on Tiananmen Square, and on June 4 those units attacked. No one knows how many hundreds of people were killed. U.S. television could not show the slaughter. Chinese officials saw to it that the attack took place under cover of darkness. Once the area around Tiananmen Square had been cleared, the demonstrators in the square itself fled. Their encampments were razed by army bulldozers. Later the government flatly denied that these events had ever occurred, a claim we will look at more closely in Chapter Ten.

The range of choices in television is also available in the other media. The hourly news updates on the radio are mere headline summaries, and all-news radio is little more. But public radio, like public television, provides in-depth news programming, including "Monitor Radio," produced by the *Christian Science Monitor* newspaper, and the daily "All Things Considered." Media critics regard both as serious journalism.

Commercial radio also has talk shows, many of which invite listeners to call in with questions and comments for the guest. Such shows vary in quality. Some attract callers whose only aim seems to be to air personal gripes and grievances, but others can be informative and even influential. When an Exxon Oil Company tanker ran aground off Alaska in 1989, spilling 11 million gallons of crude oil and polluting a huge area of fishing grounds and scenic coastline, a Washington radio talk-show host organized a nationwide anti-Exxon campaign. A few months earlier, consumer advocate Ralph Nader telephoned another talk-show host to complain about a proposed 51 percent pay hike for members of Congress and other federal officials. The complaint was picked up by hosts in other cities, and an outraged public helped put an end to the pay raise proposal.

As for America's newspapers, they range from publications like the serious and weighty *New York Times* to the colorful *USA Today* and such supermarket checkout fare as the *National Enquirer*. The choice is up to the reader. Readers also have a wide choice of books and magazines. They can pick a general news magazine like *Time* or *Newsweek*, a business publication like *Forbes* or *Business Week*, or a science journal such as *Scientific American*. They can decide whether they want a news magazine with a conservative slant, such as *The National Review*, or one with a more liberal point of view, *The Nation*, or *The New Republic* perhaps. Libraries in large cities contain millions of volumes, some available for circulation, others for research purposes only.

Add up all the books, magazines, newspapers, and radio and television stations, and the result is an abundance of media outlets — enough to keep information flowing freely.

Or is it enough? That's a good question. For despite the number of information sources available to Americans, and in spite of their seeming diversity, many critics regard our media choices as more limited than they appear.

One limit stems from the fact that although readers, listeners, and viewers have many media outlets to choose from, those outlets often seem to speak with a single voice. It's not unusual for the country's leading news magazines to highlight the same story or person in the same week, for example. Just check out the covers of *Time, Newsweek,* and *U.S. News & World Report*. Read a story in the daily paper and you're likely to come across it again in *Time* and on the evening news. In a way that's natural. If terrorists hijack an airliner or a European head of state dies, every news organization will cover the event.

However, the media's choruslike tendencies go beyond each day's top headline to include more general themes. One former head of CBS News, Van Gordon Sauter, refers to TV news as "cookie-cutter" broadcasting, and other parts of the media could be described in much the same way. In the early 1980s, for example, it was almost impossible to pick up a newspaper or magazine, or to turn on the radio or television, without hearing about missing children. News columns, editorial pages, evening news broadcasts, docudramas — the subject was everywhere. By all accounts, one and a half million American boys and girls under age thirteen were vanishing each year. As it turned out, however, that figure was grossly exaggerated, and by mid-decade, talk of missing children had all but disappeared from the media. Now everyone was discussing the sexual abuse of children. Later, media attention began veering in the direction of the disease acquired immune deficiency syndrome, or AIDS.

Never is the media lockstep more apparent than during a presidential election campaign. Campaign reporting sometimes seems to amount to an issue-of-the-week consensus, with journalists throughout the media talking about the same thing in the same way and at the same time. If what they were talking about were serious — the candidates' positions on the environment, taxes, prison reform, and so forth — that would be fine. But increasingly, say critics like Kathleen Hall Jamieson, professor of communications at the University of Texas at Austin, the media concentrate on campaign tactics rather than issues. At one time every reporter in the country is comparing the effectiveness of each candidate's television ads. Then, as if by agreement, that subject is dropped and the focus shifts to the candidates' differing abilities to relate to crowds and then to their personal styles or mannerisms. Surely, the critics say, voters ought to be able to open a paper or tune in the news and get more valuable information than that.

Actually they could. Most simply don't. And that's another limit — a self-imposed one this time — on the news and information Americans receive. If people read every page of the *New York Times* every day, the amount they would learn might astonish them. The *Times* editors describe the publication as "the newspaper of record" and take pride in printing every word of major presidential speeches, reproducing important international agreements in full, and so on. If everyone also watched PBS's "MacNeil-Lehrer Newshour" each weekday evening, tuned in to "Monitor Radio" or "All Things Considered" while driving home from work or school, and spent Sundays glued to the network talk shows, the nation would be well informed indeed.

But it's hard to imagine anyone doing all that. Just the thought of wading through the entire four sections of the daily *New York Times* is daunting. Even faithful readers refer to the paper as "the great gray *Times*" and admit to skimming over much of it. A person who read each edition front to back and also took in several hours of serious broadcast news daily would have precious little time left over for anything else. So people make choices.

Relatively few choose public broadcasting or the *New York Times*. Daily circulation for the *Times* is just over a million, while figures from the Nielsen Media Research company, which collects and analyzes television viewing data, show that sets in about 3 million households tune in to "MacNeil-Lehrer" regularly. The most popular news magazine is *Time*, with a weekly circulation of 4.6 million. *The National Review, The Nation,* and *The New Republic* do not even appear in the *World Almanac* list of leading magazines, indicating that they have circulations under 300,000. The shrieking headlines of the tabloid *National Enquirer,* by contrast, attract 4.3 million buyers weekly. But Americans' number-one reading choice is *TV Guide*. Its circulation was close to 17 million in 1987.

That choice offers a clue to Americans' choice for news: commercial network television. According to Nielsen, over 10 million households are tuned in to a twenty-two-minute newscast each evening, three times the number for "MacNeil-Lehrer." The primary news medium for a majority of Americans turns out to be one that even Walter Cronkite, who did much to pioneer that medium, calls "not adequate."

So why choose it? Because it's lively, colorful, professionally packaged, and not very demanding. It's the flair and drama of commercial television news that attract so many. The evening news is more than a source of information; it's entertainment too. ''Infotainment'' is the word media critics have coined for this particular blend of fact and fun.

5

Information, Infotainment, and the Bottom Line

"Infotainment" describes much of what passes for fact in commercial broadcasting and accounts for a great deal of the superficiality of radio and television news and information programming. Beyond that, broadcasting's commitment to infotainment values — a commitment most media observers agree grows yearly — means that Americans are getting an increasingly distorted view of reality. To see how, consider the docudrama.

Docudramas are a relatively new television form, one that represents a variation on the news documentaries of the 1960s and 1970s. Those earlier documentaries addressed serious issues: hunger in America, the plight of the nation's migrant workers, the threatened extinction of animal species, and so forth. The shows contained facts and figures, and accuracy was important. Their appeal was intellectual and their effect frequently depressing.

Docudramas are different. In them, fact is softened by fiction. Docudramas target the emotions and seek effects by shocking audiences or inspiring them. Many involve a sensational crime — the brutal murder of a wealthy young woman by a casual date in New York City's Central Park, for instance. Others target a social problem — rape, incest, and child abuse are popular — or someone coping courageously with a terrible illness. AIDS was the docudrama disease of choice as the 1990s began.

Docudramas have been charged with falsifying reality all along the line. Many that focus on social problems are criticized for magnifying those problems and making them seem more common than they are. The docudrama obsession with the "problem" of "millions" of missing children stands as an example of such overstatement. Doctors and other health workers say that docudramas about AIDS gloss over the facts of the disease and disseminate misinformation about how it spreads. Other docudramas distort historical and political events. One that did was a 1989 CBS production, "Guts and Glory: The Rise and Fall of Oliver North."

North, a former U.S. Marine Corps colonel, was real enough. In the early 1980s he was recruited by the administration of President Ronald Reagan to carry out two secret missions. The first was part of an attempt to win the freedom of several Americans being held hostage by terrorists in the Middle East. North's assignment: sell U.S. weapons to the terrorists' allies in Iran. The administration's hope was that the Iranians would then persuade the terrorists to free the Americans.

Oliver North's second covert mission was connected to his first. He was to use the profits from the arms sale to help try to overthrow the government of the Central

American nation of Nicaragua. Since 1979 that government had been a socialist one and friendly to the Soviet
Union. Reagan, convinced that the Soviets had plans to
use Central America as a staging ground for an attack
against the United States, was eager to see Nicaragua
under the control of a pro-American regime.

North accepted the assignments even though he knew
that both involved illegal activities. The weapons were
sent to Iran and two hostages were released, but others
were promptly seized in their stead. Years later they and
most of the original hostages were still in captivity. At
least one had been murdered. The proceeds from the arms
sale went to anticommunist rebels in Nicaragua. Once
again, however, the administration's hopes were not met.
When Reagan left office in 1989, Nicaraguan socialists
still held power.

When North's clandestine activities became public
knowledge in 1986, he and several others were ordered to
stand trial. By the time CBS aired "Guts and Glory," the
one-time Marine was already facing a judge and jury in a
Washington, D.C., courtroom. He freely admitted to his
actions but added that he had simply been following orders from the White House. Never at any point had it
occurred to him that he might be doing anything wrong,
North maintained.

In CBS's version of history, however, North *was*
forced to consider the legality and morality of his actions.
The actor playing North was shown discussing the ethics
of selling arms to terrorists with a character called Aaron

Sykes. North and Sykes were later depicted debating the rights and wrongs of using the proceeds of the illegal sale to try to topple a foreign government. In truth, however, no such person as Aaron Sykes ever existed.

Why the invention? "We needed . . . dramatically to give voice to those who knew what North was doing and did not approve," the show's writer explained. But the point was that there were no such people. Or, if there were, they never spoke up. What happened to North happened precisely because he was never challenged in this way. If he or someone around him had questioned his orders, his story might have turned out differently. Convicted on three charges, North was fined and sentenced to probation.

Television critics make no secret of their uneasiness over the distortions in docudramas like "Guts and Glory." And most of them expressed shock when, early in the 1989–90 television season, the networks introduced docudrama techniques into the newsroom. ABC's "Prime Time Live," NBC's "Yesterday, Today and Tomorrow," and CBS's "Saturday Night With Connie Chung" mixed dramatic reenactments of reported news events with actual news footage. ABC even used the mix on its regular evening program "World News Tonight." Critic Gore Vidal deplored these "flashing fictions," and Fred Friendly called such reporting a "fraud." Even some television executives expressed reservations about the format.

The trend toward news as entertainment is as evident

in publishing as in broadcasting. According to Hall's Editorial Reports, which keeps tabs on the content of magazines, *Time* and *Newsweek* devoted 30 percent of their editorial space to national affairs in 1980, and *U.S. News & World Report* 50 percent. Seven years later, national affairs took up only about 28 percent of *U.S. News* and 25 percent of *Time* and *Newsweek*. The rest of each magazine had been given over to "soft" news — book, play, and movie reviews, fashion news, lifestyles, and so on. As for newspapers, *USA Today* began publishing in 1980 especially to offer readers what its founder called "the journalism of hope." Even the great gray *Times* isn't as gray as it used to be, with more photos and special sections on the home, arts and leisure, "living," sports, and popular science.

Why are the media moving so determinedly in the direction of infotainment? There are any number of specific reasons, but they all boil down to a matter of dollars and cents. Readers, listeners, and viewers like infotainment. They prefer it to straight information, as Nielsen data, like newspaper and magazine circulation figures, prove. And generally, the more people who watch a show or buy a publication, the more business and industry will pay to advertise their products or services during the program or on the magazine's pages.

If circulations and Nielsen "ratings" are high, advertisers pay plenty. Thirty seconds of evening prime time on television can cost an advertiser $200,000. Television advertising giants like Procter & Gamble, Sears, General

Motors, and McDonald's spend hundreds of millions of dollars every year to air their sales pitches. In 1988 the K-Mart chain of discount stores was putting $200 million a year into newspaper advertising circulars. Naturally, media owners are willing to turn information into infotainment if doing so will attract audiences — and advertisers.

That willingness does much to shape the news and information the public sees and hears. At their 1988 annual convention, members of the American Society of Newspaper Editors agreed that it has become common practice to coordinate special sections with their advertising departments. For example, local clothing stores may be invited ahead of time to take out ads in a spring or fall fashion insert. In fact, the insert may have been planned especially to give retailers an incentive to buy extra advertising space. According to David Burgin, editor of the Houston, Texas, *Post,* publishers are particularly eager to run "upscale" articles, such as articles about fashions or vacations to exotic places, because they attract profitable upscale advertising. But if newspaper columns are filled with the upscale, something else may have to be squeezed out. "You write about the chic and the trendy and the jet-setters," Burgin says, "and you don't do as much as you would about human pain and suffering."

Sometimes advertising pressures sweep a story off the news pages altogether. The American tobacco industry, for example, has contrived to keep much of the media silent on the bad news about smoking and lung disease. The Philip Morris cigarette company once got an English court to issue an order preventing CBS's "60 Minutes" from airing an antismoking film. An English court was involved because the film had been made in London. A twelve-year study of a dozen leading U.S. women's magazines — most of which run frequent articles related to health and safety issues — turned up only twelve articles about the hazards of smoking. Half of those appeared in *Good Housekeeping,* the only publication in the group that refuses cigarette ads. When, a few years ago, the *Wall Street Journal* investigated links between tobacco advertising and editorial policy, it reported that "any big advertiser can, to a degree, blunt negative publicity about its product."

In addition to affecting what information the public gets or doesn't get, business concerns can also determine when the public gets it. Take, for example, these dates: December 1987 and January 27, 1988.

In December 1987 a group of American university scientists, funded through the National Institutes of Health (NIH), ended a several-year study of the effect of aspirin on patients with heart disease. The halt came, the scientists said, after their work showed that taking aspirin reduces the risk of having a second heart attack. So conclusive was the evidence, they added, that it would have been a waste of time to continue the project.

January 27, 1988, was the day the *New England Journal of Medicine,* one of the nation's most highly respected medical reviews, broke the story about aspirin and heart disease. Although many scientists, government officials, business leaders, and journalists had known of the findings for weeks, the potentially life-saving information had been kept from the public. Why the delay? *Journal* editors said they had needed the time to check the study's accuracy. Others, pointing out that the NIH had been convinced of its accuracy for weeks, saw a different reason. Lawrence K. Altman, medical writer for the *New York Times,* pointed to "a relatively new motive in medical journalism, the desire for newsworthiness." The desire, Dr. Altman continued, is "related to the need to make profits."

Profits for whom? The *New England Journal of Medicine* and its staff were one possibility. But other businesses and individuals also stood to gain. While heart patients remained in the dark about how aspirin might benefit them, people in the know were investing their money in companies that manufacture the drug. What was more, the delay gave aspirin makers a chance to prepare advertising campaigns timed to coincide with the *Journal*'s January 27 release date. "Recent news of a government-funded study linking aspirin with reduced risk of heart attacks caught wide public attention," wrote Robert C. Cowan, science writer for the *Christian Science Monitor,* on February 2. "But did you also notice the slick, well-prepared aspirin ads that often accompanied the news reports?"

There is another, less direct, way in which advertising

affects news and information, especially on television. When viewers don't like a particular program, they may threaten to organize a consumer boycott against the companies that advertise on it. The threat is a potent one; as the *New York Times* has said, "The way to the networks' hearts is through their pocketbooks." Boycott threats have come from many groups and individuals, and though most boycotts target entertainment programming (which, after all, comprises the bulk of the broadcast day), some have been aimed at informational offerings. "The Day After," a 1983 TV movie about the effects on an ordinary American town of a nuclear war with the Soviet Union, was the object of a boycott threat from the Moral Majority, a conservative Christian and militantly anticommunist organization. Blacks have protested the way slavery has been depicted in historical dramas. Even public, noncommercial, television may face a boycott of sorts. In 1989 Jewish groups called for individuals to stop making contributions to New York's public WNET-TV after the station announced plans to broadcast a documentary that the groups considered anti-Jewish.

Business concerns not directly related to advertising can also have an impact upon the kind and quality of information available to the public. Between 1986 and 1988 two Atlanta, Georgia, newspapers, the *Constitution* and the *Journal,* carried a number of hard-hitting investigative articles about such influential local corporations as Coca-Cola and Georgia Power Company. Eventually managers at the newspapers' parent company called editor Bill Kovach into their offices and ordered him to replace the critical stories with briefer, lighter pieces. Kovach refused but, in an apparent victory for Georgia business interests, soon handed in his resignation. The next year Kovach was named curator of Harvard University's highly regarded Nieman Foundation journalism program.

If some business pressures are applied to keep information *away* from the public, others are employed to get information *to* the public, to ensure that people are exposed to a particular point of view. The story behind the NBC docudrama "Shootdown" shows how reality may be shaped by corporate interests.

"Shootdown," aired in 1988, was the story of the downing five years earlier of a Korean airliner by the Soviet Union. The plane was over Soviet territory at the time of the shooting. Two hundred sixty-nine people, sixty-three of them Americans, perished in the tragedy. Why had it occurred? The Soviets claimed that the plane had been on a spy mission, possibly with the cooperation of the United States. The United States and Korea, on the other hand, maintained that the plane had strayed into Soviet airspace by accident and that it had been shot down deliberately and in cold blood.

In its original form "Shootdown" questioned the U.S. version of events. The script centered on the real-life mother of one of the American victims, a woman who had listened to government explanations and found them unconvincing. She called publicly for Congress to investigate the incident to see whether spying, and a subsequent coverup, had indeed been involved. As first written, the script suggested that the mother's suspicions might well have been founded in fact.

But that was not the version of the script that ended up being taped for television. According to the *New York Times,* it was "reported" that General Electric, the company that owns NBC, "insisted" on changes. With the changes, the script indicated that the mother was wrong and U.S. officials right. General Electric, the *Times* went on, is a major supplier for the U.S. Department of Defense (DOD). The implication was that company executives may have demanded the script changes because they wanted to keep on the good side of DOD officials who hand out and pay for defense contracts. The result for viewers, wrote *Times* television critic John J. O'Connor, was "confusion." He and others were disturbed by this example of editorial standards bowing to commercial interests, but they did not expect a different outcome if a similar situation arose in the future. The media's preoccupation with the "bottom line" — dollars and cents — would again dictate script changes, they were sure.

Concern for the bottom line helps explain another television trend of the late 1980s, toward a new type of programming that critics unhesitatingly dubbed "trash TV." Examples included "A Current Affair" — a program usually described as a *National Enquirer* of the airwaves — and "America's Most Wanted," a show that dramatized notorious unsolved crimes and urged viewers to be on the lookout for suspects in those crimes. Characterized by critics as a "rape and murder replay show," "America's Most Wanted" nonetheless found an audience of 22 million in its first season. It also performed a public service, or so its producers claimed. According to them, forty-eight fugitives from justice were captured after being featured on the show.

Programs like "America's Most Wanted," and such infotainment talk shows as "Donahue" and "Geraldo," have their defenders on other grounds. Van Gordon Sauter, formerly of CBS News, contends that despite appearances to the contrary, these programs are a form of journalism. "Not the capital J variety," he concedes, not the kind favored by people he calls "elitists" at newspapers like the *Washington Post* and the *New York Times.* But, Sauter went on in an article that appeared, perhaps predictably, in *TV Guide,* the shows "can be great fun. Sometimes they are relevant." If the elitists want to criticize something, he says, let them stick to network news broadcasts, which offer "identical news in an identical fashion with identical anchors." Let them focus on "developing new forms of capital J journalism that are more relevant, understandable and beneficial to the viewers." Sauter predicts they won't, though. The network broadcasting trend toward cookie-cutter reporting, sensationalism, and news as entertainment is expected to continue into the 1990s. So is the overall media slide from information into infotainment.

Another trend expected to continue — and accel-

erate — between now and the turn of the century has to
do with ownership of the media, which is becoming increasingly concentrated in the hands of a few. At a time
when there are more news and information outlets than
ever before (although the number of daily newspapers
declined from 1,657 at the beginning of 1987 to 1,645 at
the end), there are fewer owners. The main reason: mergers and buyouts. In recent years Japan's Sony Corporation bought CBS Records; a West German concern
purchased another record company as well as the Dou-
bleday and Bantam Books publishing companies; Rupert
Murdoch, owner of newspapers and broadcast stations in
England and Australia, as well as book publishing
houses, snapped up a number of media outlets, including
Triangle Publications and 20th Century Fox Film. According to Ben H. Bagdikian, retired dean of the Graduate School of Journalism at the University of California
in Berkeley, fifty corporations controlled U.S. communications in 1983. Within four years that number had
fallen to twenty-nine.

By 1989, it had dropped further, and in March of that
year came the most stupendous deal of all. Time Incorporated, already the publisher of *Time, People,* and other
magazines, and owner of various properties from Home
Box Office cable to trade and textbook publishers to
Book-of-the-Month Club to Time-Life Home Video, announced plans to merge with Warner Communications
Incorporated, which possessed, among other things,
Warner Brothers Records and TV, Electra/Asylum/

Nonesuch Records, and *Mad Magazine*. The result of the merger was an $18 billion media conglomerate, the biggest in the world.

The biggest up to then. Shortly before the deal was struck Nicholas Nicholas, Jr., president of Time, Inc., predicted that by the year 2000, "there will emerge, on a worldwide basis, six, seven, eight . . . media and entertainment megacompanies." These companies, reported Steve Lohn of the *New York Times,* "will be able to produce and distribute information and entertainment in virtually any medium: books, magazines, news, television, movies, videos, cinemas, electronic data networks and so on." Some companies may be even bigger than the new Time-Warner.

What effect will billion-dollar media megacompanies have on the right to know? Even Time-Warner officials acknowledge there may be problems. According to Nicholas, ensuring "the ability of journalists to be truly independent" could be one. Critics of the deal say the problem has already appeared. The new company's management ordered *Time* not to cover the merger story, and its editorial staff obeyed. Not until after a report appeared in rival *Newsweek* did management relent. How, a writer for the *Nation* asked sarcastically, can we expect *Time* movie critics to review Warner films?

Other questions must be considered. How, for example, will the media giants of the future react to pressure from commercial interests? Ten years from now it won't be a question of a few magazines bowing to the demands of the tobacco industry or network producers agreeing to a few script alterations to please a defense contractor. By then dozens of magazines and all the papers in the whole region of the country may be owned by one company. The same company may also own radio and television stations and book publishing houses. Although in the 1980s government rules prevented a single person or group from owning a newspaper and a broadcast facility in the same city, or a network and a cable operation from owning each other, some media experts expected those rules to be overturned in the 1990s.

There are still more questions. If dozens of media outlets sounded like a chorus in the 1980s, how will they sound by the end of the century, when all belong to the same six — or maybe eight — corporations? How will corporations that combine information and entertainment functions handle the trend away from serious news and toward reality-twisting docudramas and trash TV? Won't information be swept away in a tidal wave of infotainment? Can small-circulation publications like *The National Review* and *The Nation* survive in a world of megacompanies — and megadollars? What will it mean to have just eight — or maybe only six — companies operating on a global scale? Eight — or maybe six — giant corporations deciding which stories will go into their newspaper columns — and which won't. Eight — or six — boards of directors deciding what sorts of books to publish — and what not to publish. Eight — or six — chairmen of the board deciding which movies to distribute, which new magazines to introduce, which TV and radio programs to produce. Eight — six? — media giants controlling radio and television broadcasting in the absence of a fairness doctrine.

To see what it might be like to live in this world of a tiny number of media megaconglomerates, we need look no further than public schools in towns and cities all across America. Everyone knows what can happen when a small group of self-styled censors undertakes to decide what students and others may and may not see and read. Classics like J. D. Salinger's *The Catcher in the Rye* and Mark Twain's *Huckleberry Finn* are pulled from library shelves. Judy Blume's novels disappear as well. The censors study textbooks carefully; only those with few, if any, references to U.S. slavery, this country's warfare on its Native American population, and other touchy subjects are allowed in classrooms. The right to know of every student in the school diminishes as a result. Will the larger public's right to know diminish similarly in the future?

The media: numerous, varied, independent, rich, and powerful enough to assure Americans' continued right to know? Or so rich and powerful, and so eager to become more so, that they will become fewer and fewer, lose their variety and independence — and with that loss forfeit their position as conveyers of essential information in a democratic society?

6

Today's Headlines — Tomorrow's News

It was a dramatic scene, and CBS television cameras were on hand to record it. Four men in uniform and carrying weapons leaning over two men in ragged civilian dress, beating and kicking them as they lay helpless on the ground. The four in uniform were soldiers of the Israeli army. The unarmed civilians were Palestinian Arabs. Aired over U.S. television in February 1988, the footage from the violence-torn Middle East shocked the nation.

Not that Middle Eastern violence was anything new. The rivalries among the various peoples of the region date back to biblical times, and Jews and Arabs have been at each other's throats since the Arabs conquered the area in 636 A.D. In this century the conflict has centered around the Jewish state of Israel. Carved out of the ancient land of Palestine under the direction of the United Nations, Israel became an independent nation in 1948. For the first time since their suppression nearly 1,900 years before under the Roman emperors, Jewish people had a national home. No longer would they be hounded from place to place by religious prejudice and racial hatred. No longer would they face the threat of persecution, a threat most recently turned into reality by the leaders of Nazi Germany. During the twelve years of Nazi rule, from 1933 until the end of World War II in 1945, six million Jews perished in Europe.

From the start there was trouble between the new nation of Israel and its Arab neighbors. People in Egypt, Syria, Jordan, and other Arab countries resented the division of Palestine and resented even more seeing their fellow Arabs turned overnight into a minority in their own homeland. The fact that Israel respected the rights of its Arab citizens, allowing them to worship freely, vote, use their own language, and run their own schools, did not lessen the resentment. Arab-Israeli wars broke out in 1948, 1956, 1967, and 1973.

In the 1967 fighting Israel seized land from Egypt and Jordan. Israeli leaders later returned some Egyptian territory, but continued to hang onto Egypt's Gaza Strip and Jordan's so-called West Bank. It was on the West Bank that the 1988 beatings took place. They came three months after young Palestinians there and in Gaza began an uprising, which they called the *intifada,* aimed at forcing Israel to withdraw from the occupied areas. Armed with stones, iron bars, axes, knives, and gasoline bombs, angry Palestinians let fly at Israelis every chance they got.

Israel responded to the violence with more violence. Beatings were only part of it. Soldiers were ordered to use clubs, tear gas, and rubber bullets — and real ones, too — against the rioters. By the time the intifada had been going on for a year and a half, about two dozen Israelis and over five hundred Palestinian men, women, and children had been killed.

Israel's harsh response to the uprising dismayed Americans, most of whom were used to thinking of Israelis as the "good guys" in the Middle East. The United States and Israel have always been close. Moved by Jewish suffering during the Nazi years, America championed the establishment of the new state. Many Americans have relatives in Israel or have visited there. Americans and Israelis have political ties as well. Israel is the Middle East's only democracy, and Americans identify with it on that score. The world balance of power plays a part, too. When tensions rise in the Middle East, the United States automatically backs Israel. The Arab nations get support from the Soviet Union. For its part, Israel stands up for U.S. interests in the area. American aid to Israel is generous — $3 billion in 1988, more than the United States gives any other country. For these reasons and more, Americans and Israelis feel they share a special relationship.

Now, though, television coverage of the intifada was threatening that relationship. Each new report seemed to reinforce the image of heavily outfitted Israeli soldiers bullying youngsters armed only with whatever they could pick up from the streets of their towns and villages. American tourism to Israel dropped off. Newspaper editorials denounced Israel's reaction as excessive and urged its leaders to give up Gaza and the West Bank, to exchange "land for peace." Some suggested that the United States rethink its $3 billion a year commitment to Israel, rethink perhaps the whole alliance. Others speculated that strains between this country and its Middle Eastern ally might damage U.S. interests in that part of the world while boosting Soviet influence. If any of those things happen, today's headlines will have helped shape tomorrow's news.

It wouldn't be the first time. In the 1950s and early 1960s, the United States became involved in a war in the Southeast Asian nation of Vietnam. At the time Vietnam was divided into communist North Vietnam and noncommunist South Vietnam. However, South Vietnam's government was under attack from rebels within the country as well as from North Vietnamese troops. Seeking to save that government, the United States sent money, weapons, and military advisers to South Vietnam. By 1964 it was also sending combat soldiers. In all, nearly nine million Americans served in Vietnam. About 50,000 died.

As time passed, some Americans came to believe that their country ought not to be involved in this way. They pointed out that U.S. intelligence sources indicated that up to 80 percent of the South Vietnamese favored union with the North and a communist way of life. It was wrong, these critics said, for America to be telling people halfway around the world what kind of government they must have. At first, few listened to such talk, but when the protesters took to the streets in noisy and sometimes violent demonstrations, the media began to pay attention. Media coverage allowed the protesters to get their antiwar message across to more people — and the more who heard it, the more who began to understand and agree with it. By the early 1970s most Americans had concluded that the United States should get out of Vietnam, and in 1973 it did. Today Vietnam is a single, communist nation.

Not only may media coverage have helped hasten the U.S. withdrawal by publicizing the views of antiwar protesters, it also gave Americans a glimpse of what that war was like. That glimpse was delivered most powerfully by television. Never before had people been able to sit back in their living rooms and watch their young people fighting, bleeding, and dying, close up and in color. Nor had Americans ever had the opportunity to see other Americans shooting civilians, burning whole villages suspected of being rebel hiding places, or spraying human beings with napalm, a sticky form of gasoline that clings to the body and burns. People had read or heard about the horrors of earlier wars, of course, but words, spoken or written, lack television's visual impact. By showing the Vietnam War in its awful reality, television may have helped turn Americans against it.

There is no "may" about the role that news reporting played during the 1950s and 1960s as black Americans struggled to win such basic civil liberties as the rights to vote and use public facilities like restaurants and swimming pools. When the civil rights movement began, its leaders found themselves in the position of anti–Vietnam War protesters a decade later: with a message and few listeners. So they took to the nation's streets — a tactic the protesters of the war later borrowed from the civil rights movement. Blacks, and those whites who joined the cause, organized demonstrations and marched together, holding banners and placards and singing or chanting slogans. And they staged nonviolent "sit-ins" at lunch counters and other places with "Whites Only" signs.

The demonstrators' nonviolence was not always matched by local authorities. In 1963 firemen in Birmingham, Alabama, aimed their hoses at a group of civil rights marchers, knocking them to the ground with high-pressure streams of water. When this failed to break up the protest, the police brought in trained dogs and ordered them to attack. Newspaper photos and TV shots of the events in Birmingham — the unresisting demonstrators, the snarling, biting dogs, and the hate-filled faces of police and firemen engaged in official violence — outraged much of the nation and prompted President John F. Kennedy to ask Congress to enact a civil rights bill. The bill became law in June 1964, the year after Kennedy was killed by an assassin. Later in 1964 news of the brutal killings of three young men working in Mississippi for black voting rights spurred Congress to pass the Voting Rights Act of 1965.

Perhaps the clearest example of headlines dictating

events occurred at the end of the last century and involved newspaper magnates William Randolph Hearst and Joseph Pulitzer. Between them the two created a war and maneuvered the United States into fighting it.

As a matter of fact, Hearst and Pulitzer were not so much interested in war as they were in publishing warlike headlines. Sensationalism was their stock in trade, their way of trying to attract larger readerships. And what could be more sensational than headlines that told of battle, glory, and patriotic sacrifice? As Pulitzer himself put it, he "rather liked the idea of a war — not a big one — but one which would arouse interest and give . . . a chance to gauge the reflex in circulation figures." So editorial minds began casting about for places with potential for conflict, and they found one: the Spanish island of Cuba, off Florida.

Spanish rule in Cuba was not exceptionally severe by colonial standards (compared, for instance, with European practice in Africa and India, or with U.S. treatment of its Native Americans. The Spanish government was inept, however, and some Cubans were agitating for independence. Spanish authorities reacted by rounding up troublemakers and placing them in concentration camps. The camps were not pleasant places, but the headlines Hearst and Pulitzer produced turned the unpleasant into the lurid. The columns beneath the headlines went further, with grisly details of invented atrocities and descriptions of a Cuban war for independence that did not exist. To lend verisimilitude, the stories were illustrated with drawings, since this was before the day of newspaper photographs. When an artist hired by Hearst and dispatched to Cuba to produce the needed illustrations protested that no war was going on, Hearst is said to have cabled back, "You furnish the pictures, I'll furnish the war!" The publisher later denied sending any such message.

Whether he did or not, war came. On February 15, 1898, the U.S. battleship *Maine* blew up in Havana harbor and 260 crew members perished. The harbor may have been mined by the Spanish, or the explosion could have been caused by a malfunction on board ship. To this day no one is sure what happened. Hearst, though, never allowed his readers to question Spain's responsibility for the act, and he made "Remember the *Maine*!" a national war cry. Congress and President William McKinley called for U.S. intervention in Cuba, and in April the Spanish-American War began. It lasted until August. The victorious United States came away with three former Spanish colonies: Puerto Rico, Guam, and the Philippine Islands. Cuba gained its independence.

What Hearst and Pulitzer did in regard to Cuba and the Spanish-American War was reprehensible, of course. With a blatant disregard for the truth, the two ordered up stories that led to violence and sent thousands to their deaths. If the story of the events leading up to the Spanish-American War demonstrates anything, it is how much more responsible the U.S. press is now than it was in the past. To be sure, today's headlines may influence tomorrow's news, but at least those headlines are factual and accurate. We can count on them to reflect events as they really happen.

Or can we? A great many Israelis watching news reports of the Palestinian intifada did not think so. As they saw it, those reports distorted reality and created a potential for conflict as surely as Hearst's and Pulitzer's did. The methods were just more subtle.

Take the CBS report about Israeli soldiers beating Palestinians on the West Bank. Israeli authorities banned the original footage from the country's state-run television network, allowing only an edited version to be shown. Why the censorship? Didn't Israeli citizens have a right to know what was happening in the occupied territories?

They did, the authorities conceded, but that right was not served by coverage like CBS's. Not that CBS had lied about the actual beatings, they added. They had taken place, and the Israeli military was quick to discipline the soldiers involved. Nor did people in Israel's government suspect CBS of having staged the scene. Nevertheless, they claimed, the film was not an accurate portrayal of conditions in Gaza and the West Bank. Both places were generally peaceful, with violence the exception, not the rule. The beating incident, Israeli leaders maintained, was an event taken out of context and magnified by television in a way that obscured the realities of the Middle East situation.

The real story, they said, began more than forty years earlier, when Israel's Arab neighbors vowed to destroy the Jewish state. Four times the Arabs staged concerted invasions aimed at doing just that. Defending itself in the course of one of those invasions, Israel seized large areas of Arab territory, some of which was later returned. That was the background. The story in 1988 was that Israel might decide to keep Gaza and the West Bank permanently, partly as a buffer against future Arab incursions and partly as a means of restoring their land's ancient borders. With an eye to the possibility of annexation, Israeli leaders were already working on plans to allow Palestinians in those areas to have limited self-government.

But not much of this background was getting into the media, Israelis complained. Violence and confrontations were receiving all the notice. As a result Israel had been put in a bad light and its relations with the United States jeopardized. The distortion of reality was especially pronounced on U.S. commercial television, the Israelis charged, as witness CBS's film of the West Bank beatings.

There may be some truth to the charge. We saw in the last chapter that network news coverage does emphasize the dramatic, often at the expense of the reasoned. That is as true of international events as it is of coverage of a plane's emergency landing as opposed to details of a new weapons system, or a president's goodbye wave to reporters in place of more information about complex climate trends. What evening news executive could resist giving airtime to a graphic display of violence, even if the limits of the twenty-two-minute broadcast make it impossible to provide a full explanation of the history and politics behind the violence?

Israeli critics raised another question about CBS's West Bank footage. Why had the beatings occurred in the first place? To say that the soldiers were retaliating against Palestinian rock throwers was only part of the answer. The other part had to do with the rock throwers themselves and with their motive for targeting those particular soldiers at that particular moment.

The motive, in the Israeli view, was to attract the attention of the CBS camera crew that happened to be nearby. According to Teddy Kollek, the Israeli mayor of Jerusalem, "A television camera is a guarantee of an immediate demonstration or riot" in the occupied lands.

Why? Palestinians living in those lands in 1988 wanted the Israelis to withdraw from the occupied territories. They knew, however, that alone they were helpless to force that withdrawal. Only if they could enlist public opinion, especially American public opinion, on their side, would they have a real chance of getting their way.

How to enlist such opinion? Even little children in Gaza and the West Bank had the answer to that one. Through network television, the main source of news and information in America. The Palestinians also understood how to mold their message to suit the medium — keep it simple and keep it visual. Never mind background. Skip the history. Forget political niceties. Concentrate on emotions instead, promoting an image of Palestinians as defenseless yet courageous in the face of overwhelming Israeli might. Lob a few stones at some soldiers. Hope they react unwisely. Let the cameras do the rest. And if the cameras don't happen to be present? Leave the rock throwing to another day. It was not that CBS staged an event, Israelis leaders concluded, it was that without the network cameras, the event might well not have taken place.

Were they right? Were television crews allowing themselves to be used by the Palestinians? Were they, not sensationalizing events as Hearst and Pulitzer had done, but allowing others to do the sensationalizing for them? Were they, not deliberately inventing conflict, but, merely by being present, encouraging its creation? Would the intifada come to an end if the seven hundred foreign reporters sent to the occupied territories at the start of the uprising packed up their cameras and headed for home?

7

Manipulation, Missing Information, and Media Responsibility

Few Americans believed that U.S. news reporting had created the Palestinian intifada or that the uprising would stop if reporters no longer covered it. Still, most conceded that news reports had helped fuel the violence. Although reporters no longer "furnish the war," they do furnish cameras, and television cameras, especially, attract events as surely as events attract reporters. As Reuven Frank, former president of NBC news, observed after viewing TV coverage of the demonstrations by Chinese students and workers in the spring of 1989, "The presence of the camera changes the nature of the event." The truth of that statement has been demonstrated, not only in Gaza and the West Bank and Beijing's Tiananmen Square, but in many other times and places. Never, though, has it been more obvious than in Tehran, the capital of Iran, between 1979 and 1981.

On November 4, 1979, anti-American Iranians seized the U.S. embassy in Tehran and held it, along with sixty-two American hostages, until January 1981. During much of that time the people of Tehran went about their business routinely and the streets around the embassy remained quiet.

But when media representatives put in an appearance, the change was instantaneous. Out of nowhere a crowd would materialize. Calm faces would take on furious expressions, and ordinary men and women would transform themselves into a howling, sign-waving mob. Many signs were written in Farsi, the language of Iran, but a fair number were in English — a tribute to the message-spreading power of the American media. The noise and confusion would continue as long as the cameras kept rolling. The minute they stopped, so did the demonstration. Signs were lowered, faces smoothed out, and the throng evaporated. Quiet would reign. Once again Iranians had used the media to get their anti-American point of view across to a world audience.

Media people have cooperated in shaping other types of events. Every time an individual or a group stages a terrorist act, such as hijacking an airplane, the terrorists can be certain that reporters will flock to the scene. They arrive and report the terrorists' demand: freedom for the passengers in exchange for whatever they happen to want — the release from prison of other terrorists, perhaps, or their own safe passage to a different part of the world. Then, in the glare of press coverage, with the world watching breathlessly, hijackers, airline officials, passengers, government spokespersons, security police, and others play out their roles — threatening, warning, pleading, bargaining. The media play their part, too, heightening the tension with on-the-spot coverage, special reports, and live updates. The drama may go on for days — or weeks. One 1985 plane hijacking began on June 14 and did not end until the thirtieth. Hijackers do not always win their specific demand, but they do get what they crave even more: publicity for their cause. And they get it in large part courtesy of the media's appetite for sensation. "A measure of the jaded standards of the media," says Jerome A. Barron, dean of the School of Law at Syracuse University, "is that when protest leaves the level of reason, broadcast time and newspaper space become abundantly available."

Closer to home, too, people have learned to manipulate the media into providing time and space to spread their message. Early civil rights leaders discovered the technique almost by accident at places like Birmingham, where officials seemed determined to treat protesters in a manner guaranteed to win them sympathy and support. After the United States became involved in Vietnam in the mid-1960s, antiwar activists, many of them veterans of the civil rights movement, deliberately tried to provoke the authorities into giving them the same sort of treatment. Their protests tended to be confrontational — especially in the presence of reporters and cameras — with demonstrators pushing, shoving, and yelling taunts at the police and others sent to keep order. Sometimes the authorities did just what protest leaders hoped they would: overreact. On May 4, 1970, four students were killed and nine wounded by national guardsmen called in to keep an eye on demonstrators at Kent State University in Ohio. The tragedy made headlines — and converts to the anti-war cause. The tactic of provocation worked, albeit at the cost of four lives. It still works today when employed from time to time by antinuclear activists, homosexual rights groups, and others.

The media help shape other types of events as well. Take elections. On the day of the 1980 U.S. presidential election, ABC, CBS, and NBC stationed pollsters outside voting places around the country. The pollsters stopped voters at random as they left the voting booths and asked which candidate — Republican Ronald Reagan or Democrat Jimmy Carter — each had chosen. Over and over the answer was Reagan. Because the election had been expected to be close, this was startling, the stuff of headlines.

Headlines it was, the minute the New York-based networks began their election night coverage. It looked as if Reagan was a shoo-in, reporters said; although it was only seven or eight P.M. Eastern Time, the result was a foregone conclusion.

But it was not seven or eight in the evening on the West Coast, it was only four or five in the afternoon, and millions of West Coasters had yet to vote. Now they were headed home from work, planning to stop at the voting booth — and what were they hearing? That the election was already over and the winner declared. So what was the point in bothering to cast their ballots? No point, a lot of them decided. The West Coast's low voter turnout did not alter the presidential results — the network pollsters were correct in saying that Reagan would have won no matter what happened there — but it did affect state and local races in California, Oregon, and Washington. Many of those who didn't vote were Democrats, disappointed that their presidential candidate had already been labeled a loser. West Coast Democratic candidates who lost in close contests blamed their defeat on TV news reports.

Eight years later, in 1988, network officials promised to withhold their exit poll predictions until voting hours were over. In New York, at least, the promise was broken. At 5:05 in the afternoon, almost four hours before the polls were to close, New York City's WNBC-TV told viewers that Democrat Michael Dukakis seemed to be winning there. Dukakis did carry New York, but across the nation he ended up losing to Republican George Bush. No one can say with certainty what effect NBC's announcement had on other races.

Another way the press may influence election results is through what is called the bandwagon effect. Suppose preelection polls show that Candidate Smith has much more support among voters than Candidate Jones. Then, two weeks before the election, Jones moves up in the polls — not very far up, but a little. If there isn't more interesting campaign news to cover, Jones's small gain becomes the media focus of the week. Suddenly, in the cookie-cutter world of American journalism, everyone is writing and talking about Jones, about her "leap" in the polls, her unexpected momentum, the possibility of a come-from-behind victory. Excitement grows. More voters throw their support to Jones — jump on her bandwagon. New polls reflect that support, and the momentum mounts. If Jones ends up winning, will it be because of her appeal to the voters? Or because media "hype" turned into a self-fulfilling prophecy? A sort of "anti-bandwagon" effect exists, too. If, after her initial spurt, Jones doesn't continue to gain in the polls — or doesn't gain as much as media prognosticators said she would — all the public will hear about is how badly she's doing, how she's about to slip, stumble, fall. . . . Such prophecies, too, can be self-fulfilling.

The media also shapes events in the world of crime. In 1988, for instance, decisions made by ABC-TV executives in New York City forced state and federal agents to change their plans for arresting illegal drug dealers in West Virginia. William Kolibash, a U.S. attorney, says he permitted an ABC camera crew to ride along in unmarked police cars to tape the activities of a group of suspected dealers. The video tape, which included a scene showing a sale of the powerful and highly addictive form of cocaine known as crack, was to be part of a network news special. Kolibash told reporters later that ABC had agreed not to air the tape until his agents and West Virginia police were ready to make their arrests. "We were kind of concerned that if some of those people saw themselves on television, they would disappear," he explained. But ABC refused to delay its broadcast. Result: the arrests came weeks ahead of schedule, before the police were fully prepared.

Press coverage influences the activities of police and criminals in other ways. It is not uncommon for people who see or read press reports about a sensational crime to be inspired to commit similar crimes themselves. In 1989 stories in the English media about a food-tampering case prompted a rash of "copycat crimes." The original crime involved bits of glass introduced into a jar of baby food. A mother who purchased the jar spotted the deadly pieces and notified the police, and the press picked up the story. After it appeared in the papers and on television, other jars of baby food in stores around the country were found to have been opened and tampered with. Police evidence, however, indicated that only the first crime was the work of the original perpetrator. The other cases almost certainly would not have occurred had the first one not been reported.

International terrorists have also been copycats. Extensive coverage of one terrorist attack may stimulate attacks by other terrorists eager to draw attention to their own causes. Still other copycats, says Lawrence Freedman of the Institute of Social and Behavioral Pathology, are people who commit terrorist-type crimes for reasons that may be unrelated to politics. Within one month in 1988 a Utah man with a religious grievance held his own family hostage for thirteen days, two people in North Carolina took over a local newspaper to protest police corruption, and a couple of men in Alabama dramatized their concern for the nation's hundreds of thousands of homeless people by seizing two teachers and twenty-six pupils at an elementary school.

Crimes motivated by racial hatred may also be set off by press reporting. News stories about black families moving into all-white public housing projects have been known to incite white bigots to violence, for instance. Others who may be impelled to action by seeing or reading news reports are people considering suicide. Clusters of suicides are especially common among teenagers, the statistics show, and reports of one act of self-destruction not uncommonly trigger others in the same community.

Are such tragedies avoidable? Should the media simply not report suicides, terrorism, demonstrations with the potential for violence, and so forth?

In a way, it is tempting to say yes. If the media refused to go on providing coverage — and free publicity — for hijackers, the hijack business would probably grind to a halt. There's not much point in seizing a plane and terrorizing its passengers unless the world is watching and worrying. And surely the media ought not to be dictating to law-enforcement agents about the timing of drug raids.

But who's to tell the media what they can and cannot publish and broadcast? Government?

In many places governments do. We saw in Chapter One that according to one study, three quarters of all governments impose some sort of censorship on the media. South Africa's white-run government censored the news media under an emergency decree issued in 1986, with the result that virtually all mention of that country's antiapartheid movement dropped out of the world press. The government of the People's Republic of China similarly enforced strict censorship in the wake of its June 4, 1989, massacre of civilians in Beijing.

Israeli leaders also turned to censorship because of the intifada. Not only did they edit the CBS clip of the 1988 West Bank beatings for home viewing, they also shut down the Arab-owned Palestinian News Service and at times barred reporters from the occupied territories. For Israel's American friends, the sight of that nation taking even a small step in the direction of censorship, following the example of nations like South Africa and China, was sad indeed. Many Israelis were equally disturbed. "Unrestricted access [to the scene of news events] . . . is a principle crucial to our democratic process," said Jerusalem's Mayor Kollek. Israelis might not like knowing, or having the world know, about Israeli brutalities in the occupied lands, but know about them they must if Israel is to maintain its democratic tradition.

But if government censorship is unacceptable or impossible in a democracy, what, if anything, should be done about the media's potential for shaping events? What, if anything, should be done about the media's vulnerability to manipulation?

One possibility is to ask people in the media to censor

themselves. This should not be too difficult for them; a lot of self-censorship is already going on. Television writers alter a script to downplay the suggestion that the U.S. government might have lied to the public about the shooting down of a Korean jetliner. Publishers ban articles that might offend local businesses or advertisers. TV producers blur the terrible realities of a disease like AIDS, and a magazine's editors delay publication of information that might have helped thousands of heart patients. Network executives replace thought-provoking documentaries with audience-grabbing docudramas.

But this kind of self-censorship is imposed in the name of profits — the bottom line. That is what makes it acceptable to media owners and managers. Is it realistic to expect those same owners and managers to restrain themselves, if doing so means ignoring a scoop or missing out on a chance to use the sensational to gain readers, listeners, and viewers? Look at how NBC fell prey to election-night temptation and revealed its exit poll prediction before voting was over in 1988. Or the way ABC refused to delay the airing of its crack-sale tape.

Anyway, is self-censorship really more desirable than the officially enforced variety? Many would argue that it is worse. At least if people outside the media are doing the censoring, those inside are going to resist them and fight to get as much information as they possibly can into print and out over the airwaves. If insiders are doing their own censoring, the battle is over before it has begun. And that would be a disaster for the public's right to know, media people say. They believe they have a responsibility not to withhold any newsworthy information, no matter how sensational it may be or how damaging it may prove to a particular nation, group, or individual. The media exist to inform people, their representatives say, and despite all the criticism, they are doing so with unprecedented power and conviction as the world enters the last decade of the twentieth century.

Defenders of the American media pointed to television coverage of the 1989 Chinese student protests as an example of excellence. Thanks to the media, and in particular to American television, the world got to see history in the making. Even *The Nation* magazine, not normally enthusiastic about the more popular press, applauded the coverage. In Tiananmen Square, its editorialists said, the media stood as a "force against injustice, exposing the reality of repression and dramatizing the depth of conviction of aggrieved citizenries." At the same time, though, *The Nation* couldn't resist pointing out that once again the media had allowed themselves to be used. Its writers prefaced their description of the media as a "force against injustice" with "unwitting," and added, "The Western media, though they would be pained to admit it, were a sideshow, an instrument of convenience for the students."

And what happened when the massacre was over, students and workers in disarray, and Beijing almost back to normal? the critics demanded. Historic events were still occurring in China. Protest leaders were being arrested, hurried through trials to predetermined guilty verdicts, and quietly executed. But in the United States, reports of these doings were slipping off the front pages and out of the consciousness of television viewers. Why? "First," wrote Gerry Boyle, columnist for the Guy Gannett newspaper chain, because "the media tend to have the attention span of a two-year-old."

And second? In the view of many, the media were in Beijing in 1989 for the same reason they went to Gaza and the West Bank in 1988, to Kent State University in 1970, to Birmingham in 1963 — and to Cuba in 1898. They were there to capitalize on the dramatic and sensational, to win viewers and subscribers with thrilling headlines and exciting stories. When the action moved from noisy streets to back rooms in government office buildings, from gallant protest to totalitarian politics-as-usual, the media appetite for sensation forced them to look elsewhere for news.

Something similar happens over and over, the critics say. The media were right on the spot in 1988 when the Alabama men upset about the homeless took hostages. But where were they back in the early 1980s, when the administration of President Ronald Reagan was making drastic 51 percent cuts in federal government spending on housing for low-income Americans? Nowhere to be seen.

Where were they in the mid 1980s, by which time homelessness had already become a pressing problem across
the nation? Again nowhere. But let twenty-six children
be seized and threatened, and the press was right on top
of the story. By 1988 the press had also gotten around to
talking about America's homeless, then estimated to
number up to three million. Perhaps, the critics say, there
wouldn't have been so many if the media had alerted the
public to the problem at the outset.

Other major stories slip by networks and publications
so obsessed with attention getting that they may overlook
the merely essential. A famine that began in Ethiopia in
1983 only came to public notice in the United States a
year later through reports from the British Broadcasting
Corporation (BBC). Once Americans knew of the disaster, they responded with aid. Shouldn't the U.S. media
be condemned for an indifference that allowed thousands
to die before that aid was forthcoming? A 1988 war between the Southeast Asian nations of Laos and Thailand
that took hundreds of lives also went largely unreported,
as did a war between Iran and Iraq that lasted most of the
1980s and left millions dead. A 1988–89 civil war in the
East African nation of Somalia, in which thousands were
killed and atrocities abounded, did not make it into the
world media, either. Might any of these conflicts have
been shortened, and casualties reduced, if coverage had
been more intense?

Very likely. No one questions that the modern mass

media can capture public happenings in almost any part of the world and bring them into our homes in ways that are immediate, compelling, and deeply moving. Critics ask only that media people do both consistently, with less regard for drama and more for underlying issues, and that they take more care to use their tremendous power to shape events and form opinion responsibly.

8

Personal Privacy, Public Awareness

On April 13, 1987, Gary Hart formally announced his candidacy for the Democratic nomination for president of the United States. Tall, dark-haired, and ruggedly handsome, the former Colorado senator had been plagued for years by rumors that he was unfaithful to his wife. Now, hoping to put an end to the stories, Hart invited members of the press to follow him day and night. Any who accepted the invitation would be "very bored," he promised.

"Bored" was not the word used by the *Miami Herald* photographers and reporters who staked out Hart's Washington, D.C., home the first weekend in May. On Sunday, May 3, the same day Hart's invitation appeared in print, they reported that the ex-senator had spent at least part of the weekend alone at the house with a woman, a Florida model who was not his wife. Hart, noting that the surveillance had been incomplete — a back door had been left unobserved — claimed the reporters had "misconstrued" events, and that the two had not been in the house overnight. His denial was to no avail. Five days later, with new details about his reputed affairs making headlines almost hourly, the would-be nominee dropped out of the race. "I refuse to submit my family . . . to further rumors and gossip," he told reporters. He also aimed some sharp criticism in their direction. During U.S. election campaigns, he told reporters, the media become hunters and the candidates the hunted.

A lot of Americans found themselves agreeing. True, Hart might be guilty of adultery. But wasn't that a personal matter and none of the press's business? Many thought so. Even many who did not, who believed they have a right to know all the details of a public person's private behavior, felt that in setting up its spy operation and stationing reporters around Hart's home the *Herald* had gone too far. Investigative reporting is one thing, they said, but "keyhole journalism" is something else. It simply is not ethical for the media to resort to such underhanded tactics to get a story.

Ethical such tactics may or may not be, but they definitely are common, and presidential aspirants are not the only ones subjected to them. In July 1987, U.S. Court of Appeals judge Robert Bork was nominated by President Reagan for a seat on the Supreme Court. Bork never served on the court because his nomination was rejected by the Senate, but before that happened, a Washington weekly called *City Paper* published a background piece on him. The story purported to be a character profile, based on an analysis of 146 movies the Bork family had rented from a local video store. Fortunately for the Borks, their tastes ran to Alfred Hitchcock thrillers and old Cary Grant classics. Even the most sensation-minded reporter or editor would have had trouble making much out of that. Give *City Paper* staffers credit for trying, though. "The inner workings of Robert Bork's mind are revealed by the videos he rents," they advertised in headline type.

On other occasions, and in pursuit of other victims, reporters have come up with more damaging information. One method they have used is to search through people's trash collections. What might they come across there? Credit card receipts, bills, empty pill containers or liquor bottles, pages from memo pads, letters, and snapshots, to name a few. It's not hard to imagine the sort of dossier a dedicated practitioner of "garbage pail journalism" can amass from a few days of digging.

Modern journalists also have at their disposal an arsenal of sophisticated electronic spy equipment. A 1988 *Time* magazine article listed some examples: "A TV camera with a pinhole-size lens concealed in an otherwise ordinary black lunch box, a microphone attached to the bottom of a wristwatch, a nightscope capable of recording television pictures in the dark and a high-resolution color camera so small that it can be hidden in the hollowed end of a racquetball racquet."

Not only are such devices in common use, most are also legal. It is not against the law to use a camera, even a hidden one, in a public place such as a street or a restaurant. Although it is illegal to record a conversation without permission from at least one of the parties to it, that rule provides little protection for a person who is the target of a reporter's inquiries. If one of the parties to a conversation is the reporter, permission is automatic. Garbage grubbing is not an illegal activity either, nor is spying on a person's home from a public road or sidewalk. Even the *City Paper* reporters who checked out the Borks' movie rentals had the law on their side. In 1988 no state or federal statute protected the privacy of video store records — or the records of most other types of businesses.

But if such intrusive reporting is both legal and common, questions remain. For example, what happens if reporters get their facts wrong, as Gary Hart claimed they did in his case? What recourse would Hart have had if the *Miami Herald* had been mistaken?

About all he could have done would have been to demand a retraction. Media managers sometimes do take back stories that prove untrue and sometimes even apologize for carrying them. A sober retraction, however, rarely gets as much attention as a sensational rumor, partly because it is less interesting and partly because it usually appears in small print on an inside page or at the end of a broadcast. The original story, even if inaccurate, tends to lead off the evening news or make the first page.

If he was innocent, Hart's only other recourse would have been to sue for libel. If he could prove his case to a judge and jury, he might have been able to collect money damages from the paper. Doing so, though, would have been tough. It is tough for anyone in the United States to prove libel, but it is especially so for politicians and other public figures, who have less legal protection than private citizens. The reason for that goes back to 1635 and the seditious libel trial of New York printer John Peter Zenger. As we saw, Zenger's acquittal established the legal principle that truth is an absolute defense against a libel charge.

Other cases, including one that ended in a 1988 Supreme Court ruling, have further established that even if what is published is not true, it is not libelous unless it can be shown to have been a deliberate, malicious lie, a lie that its creator intended people to accept as fact. In a 1989 decision a federal appeals court ruled that a reporter can go so far as to alter statements made by a public person and still not have committed libel. To demonstrate libel in his case, Hart would have had to show that the reporters had acted "with the knowledge that [what they were saying about him] was false or with reckless disregard of whether it was false or not." The reporters, on the other hand, would have had to display only "absence of malice" to be found not guilty.

When malice is found to be present, though, the verdict may be guilty even if a public figure is involved. Actress and comedian Carol Burnett won a libel suit against the *National Enquirer* after that tabloid ran an item saying, falsely, that she had been observed in public in a drunken condition. Some years later a country music star sued the tabloid *Globe* for its statement that she had nearly died from a drug overdose.

U.S. libel law is considered a bulwark of the First Amendment, and consequently of the right to know. In countries where it is easier for public officials to prove libel, as it is in England, it is also easier for those officials to silence their critics. But the fact that libel suits are so hard to win in the United States only intensifies the urgency of ethical questions about intrusive reporting. A press so thoroughly protected under the law has a responsibility to be extremely careful about balancing the public right to know against the individual right to privacy.

How careful is the U.S. press? It used to be very careful indeed. What happened to Gary Hart in 1987 would have been unthinkable twenty-five years earlier. Writing about the Hart incident a few days after it took place, *New York Times* reporter R. W. Apple recalled a similar occurrence, one that involved President John F. Kennedy. "In early 1963," he wrote, "a fledging reporter for this newspaper" — presumably himself — "was assigned to patrol the lobby of the Carlyle Hotel while President Kennedy was visiting New York City. The reporter's job was to observe the comings and goings of politicians, but what he saw was the comings and goings of a prominent actress, so that was what he reported to his editor. 'No story there,' said the editor, and the matter was dropped.'' It wouldn't be dropped today; it would be emblazoned across page one.

Why the change? Media people trace much of the reason for it back to the Watergate scandal. After the break-in at Democratic party headquarters there, most reporters meekly took President Nixon's word for it that he knew nothing about any wrongdoing. They accepted similar assurances from other leading Republicans as well. As it became more and more clear over the next two years that Nixon and the others had lied, reporters reacted with indignation — and a heightened sense of suspicion. "Watergate left us with more of a tendency to ask everything and to leave out nothing," says Bill Monroe, editor of the *Washington Journalism Review*. The *Miami Herald* reporters and photographers were acting on that tendency when they set their trap for Hart.

But even if Hart was involved in an extramarital affair, what did that have to do with the public right to know? Polls taken in the wake of the incident indicated that a majority of Americans do not regard infidelity by itself as a reason to deny a person public office. Didn't that mean reporters had created an issue where none existed? Shouldn't they have dismissed the rumors and concluded that Hart's affairs, real or imagined, were a private matter? Shouldn't they have passed up the candidate's invitation to trail him? Hadn't they, in a sense, put him "on trial" in the media?

Many people have found themselves "tried" in that way. In 1989 Jim Wright of Texas, a congressman and the speaker of the House of Representatives, was accused of having profited unethically from a book contract deal he made with business partners, friends, and political supporters. House members investigated the charge, but not before Wright had been declared guilty by much of the press and by the public at large. His resignation was a foregone conclusion. That same year baseball's Pete Rose, former batting star and manager of the Cincinnati Reds team, faced a media "trial" on charges of illegal gambling on sports events, including Reds' games. He, too, was scrutinized and found guilty in the court of public opinion, long before baseball's commissioner ruled on his actions.

Was Hart also tried in an extralegal fashion? Perhaps. But polls showed that most Americans were relieved when Hart dropped his quest for the presidency. Their reasons came down to the question of judgment. People agreed that in issuing his challenge to the press, then squiring a glamorous young woman around town, Hart had shown a lack of common sense few cared to see in the White House. It was *because* reporters had demonstrated so little restraint that the candidate's poor judgment had been revealed. Did that mean the paper had acted — even if inadvertently — in the public interest?

How are media people supposed to distinguish between what the public needs to know and what it does not? Where should they draw the line between the truly newsworthy and the merely interesting? Private misbehavior does not always affect public performance, but it can. What if Hart had become president and someone had tried to blackmail him about an indiscretion? What if the woman in the case had been, not an American model, but an official in the Soviet embassy? An involvement with such a person would really leave a president open to blackmail.

Other private lifestyles can have public implications as well: homosexuality, alcoholism, and illegal drug use, for example. On the other hand, Americans' moral and ethical standards have changed over the years, and some lifestyles no longer trouble the public as they used to. Once no self-proclaimed homosexual could have been elected to Congress. By the late 1980s at least two were regularly winning elections.

Nevertheless, most people still regard as abhorrent personal habits that would appear to have little bearing on public performance. In 1985 a member of one federal agency, the Securities and Exchange Commission, resigned his post after it became known that he had beaten his wife over an eighteen-year period. Domestic violence is terrible, but what has it to do with regulating high finance? And what, many wondered, would the media have done if the man's offense had been of a less sensational nature? What if he had had links with the businesses he was helping to regulate, or had accepted gifts from people in those businesses? Would reporters have been so eager to dig into such allegations — which, unlike wife beating, would have had a direct bearing upon the commissioner's ability to carry out his public duties?

Where should the media draw the line between the right to know and the right to privacy when it comes to a public person's history of psychiatric problems? In 1972 the Democratic party nominated Missouri senator Thomas Eagleton for vice president. He left the race after the media disclosed that he had received electric shock treatments during a bout of depression. Was that a private mental health matter unsuited to public discussion — or an issue of urgency about someone who would take over as chief executive if anything happened to the president?

What about matters of physical health? Here again, disclosure and reporting standards have changed over the years. President Woodrow Wilson suffered a stroke in the fall of 1919 and never fully recovered. For weeks — and without the nation's knowing it — the president's wife and his doctor attended to most day-to-day affairs of state. When a heart attack struck President Dwight D. Eisenhower in 1955, doctors and White House aides kept the seriousness of his condition secret. But when President Reagan underwent a cancer operation, pictures and diagrams of his intestinal tract were splashed across front pages and displayed on TV. Were such details newsworthy or just interesting? The public needs to know when its president is incapacitated. But does it need every last detail?

Does the public need to know the details of *our* personal lives, yours and mine? It can happen. Any private citizen who chances to wander into an event deemed worthy of media coverage becomes vulnerable to media tactics and techniques. Reporters have few compunctions about querying the stunned survivors of tornadoes, plane crashes, and other disasters, or about intruding on the grief of those who have just lost a loved one. "What went through your mind when you learned your son was killed by a drunk driver?" is a question newsmen and women actually ask as cameras zoom in mercilessly on a bereaved parent's face. A 1985 survey for the American Society of Newspaper Editors showed that two thirds of respondents believe reporters take advantage of the victims of circumstance. Close to 80 percent agreed that reporters do not "worry much about hurting people." Even some in the media admit they can be callous. As *Milwaukee Journal* editor Sig Gissler summed matters up: "We have a commercial interest in catastrophe."

No one is safe from catastrophe, which means no one is safe from invasion of privacy by the media. After a Texas toddler fell into an abandoned open well, reporters and television camera crews rushed to the scene of the accident. And there they stayed, issuing regular bulletins and waiting for the rescue to be accomplished. But the rescue effort took days, and to fill the time the media entertained the country with every tidbit they could dig up about the child and her family, right down to the details of her teenaged parents' stressful marriage. What informational purpose was served by making a desperately anxious couple the object of such intimate speculation?

Nor did the press appear overly solicitous for the welfare of three Florida boys infected with the AIDS virus through blood transfusions. Despite doctors' assurances that the boys presented no health threat to their classmates and neighbors, many in their community began a campaign of harassment aimed at forcing them out of town. When an arsonist burned their home to the ground, the family's move became inevitable. Some observers were shocked that the media did not hesitate to inform the world of the location of the family's new home.

Members of the media, of course, defend their reporting standards and methods. They justify resorting to miniature cameras and other spy-type equipment by pointing to situations in which such devices have been put to work in the public interest. In 1988 Philadelphia TV reporters covering the kidnaping of an infant from a local hospital armed themselves with a camera the size of a Magic Marker in order to test the hospital's security procedures. Despite the claims of hospital officials that security was adequate, the reporters were able to stroll past the visitors' desk and through the corridors of the pediatric wing, chatting with the young patients. "We were able to document very visibly that although the hospital said it had security procedures, they were in fact not being followed," the station's news director reported. Investigative journalist Pam Zekman of Chicago's WBBM-TV champions the use of spy tactics as a means of enabling the public to make judgments independent of media hype. "The more pictures you have and the more documents you can show," she maintains, "the more people can reach their own conclusions."

Journalists similarly rebut criticism of their coverage of private individuals thrust into public situations. Why shouldn't they inform the public that children infected with AIDS had moved into a particular town? they might have asked. Didn't people in that town have the right to know that the disease existed among them? What was so terrible about revealing the background of the little girl who fell down the well? Being the focus of media attention turned out happily for the child and her family. The outpouring of national sympathy — and cash — ensured her future well-being, including her college education.

As a matter of fact, media people remind their critics, a lot of people like being in the limelight, never mind the loss of privacy. Politicians like Gary Hart dote on it. Without media attention, how would they be elected to office? If politicians suffer from media overexposure, suggests reporter Peter Montgomery of *Common Cause* magazine, they have largely themselves to blame. "It is the politicians . . . who have dragged their personal lives into campaigns. Spouses and children are now standard props in the campaign production, and candidates vie for 'humanizing' television images showing their 'regular-Joe' home lives."

Many private individuals, too, bask in publicity. Some simply enjoy feeling important, but others have what they see as practical reasons for seeking publicity. The parents of a child who is desperately ill with a liver or kidney disease may use the media to beg for an organ donor, for instance. Those with a son or daughter suffering from a condition like muscular dystrophy or asthma may permit him or her to be displayed as a "poster child" for medical fund-raising purposes.

Other people, both private and public, court the attention of the media because they believe someone may benefit from learning of their personal trials and triumphs. When First Lady Nancy Reagan told reporters that she was being treated for breast cancer, thousands of women around the country who suspected they might have the disease also sought treatment. Who knows how many lives her openness — and the media's reporting of it — may have saved? Some men and women speak out about their addiction to drugs or alcohol. People like actors Jason Robards, Jr., and Elizabeth Taylor, and former First Lady Betty Ford have inspired hundreds, perhaps thousands, to face up to their own chemical dependencies and enter rehabilitation centers.

Reporters can even argue that their questioning of disaster survivors and grieving relatives of the victims of tragedy serves the public. Perhaps the personal details from the well site in Texas constituted a warning to other young people about the difficulties of early marriage and the hazards of raising children. And if showing a mother's reaction to news of her son's death in a drunk-driving accident keeps just one viewer from taking to the road — and killing someone — after drinking, doesn't that justify the reporting? Besides, representatives of some news organizations add, they strive to be fair and take precautions to avoid hurting people. At one Minnesota television station, WCCO-TV, managers have a policy of not permitting reporters to ask victims' relatives how they feel. Newspaper reporters for the Long Island, New York, *Newsday* may not visit the home of the victim of a fatal accident until relatives have been informed of the tragedy.

Most elements of the media observe another limit as well. When it comes to the crime of rape, editors and reporters are generally willing to respect the victim's privacy. According to estimates from the Institute for the Study of Applied and Professional Ethics at Dartmouth College in New Hampshire in 1989 only 5 or 10 percent of U.S. newspapers reported rape victims' names.

Much as the public may appreciate such reticence, it sits poorly with some reporters and editors. "It seems unfair to me with the presumption of innocence to report one party of a trial and not the other," mused the publisher of a Washington paper. Why, he wanted to know, should the name of the accused — who may not be guilty of any crime — be publicized, while the name of his accuser is not?

In 1983 a small weekly, the *Florida Star,* answered that question by printing the name of a woman who had been raped. It did so in violation of its own previous policy as well as in defiance of a Florida law forbidding the publication of such information. The woman sued for invasion of privacy and was awarded $100,000 in damages.

Lawyers for the *Star* challenged the decision and ap-

PERSONAL PRIVACY, PUBLIC AWARENESS   101

pealed it all the way to the Supreme Court. In 1989 the justices decided that under the First Amendment, the paper had the right to identify the woman, since her name was already a matter of public court record. The court did not rule, however, on the state law that prohibited the naming of rape victims, allowing judgment on the constitutionality of that and similar statutes to await another day. Most journalists welcomed the court's decision as a victory for their First Amendment rights.

That may have been a shortsighted view. Or rather, it may turn out to be if the media begin broadcasting and printing the names of the victims of this most intimate and personal of crimes. If rape victims see and hear their names, they and their friends, relatives, and sympathizers may react by demanding measures to limit publication. The result could be new laws intended to force the media to change the way they report on rape trials and, by extension, on other types of criminal and civil proceedings. Such laws could have a dampening effect on investigative reporting — and consequently, on the public's right to know.

Other proposed laws threaten to have such effects. After Washington's *City Paper* published its profile of Robert Bork, several members of Congress introduced bills that would protect the privacy of personal business records, such as those collected by employers, insurance companies, and retail stores, including video stores. Individual state legislatures could decide to enact privacy laws of their own. Other measures under consideration in some states would keep secret the job applications of people applying for government work or close to public scrutiny investigations into complaints against licensed professionals: electricians, psychologists, pharmacists, and others.

Another media-limiting possibility would be the repeal of so-called shield laws in states that have them. Shield laws allow reporters to keep secret the names of their sources of information and thus protect them. What sources? A government employee aware of financial irregularities in her department. A nuclear power plant technician who knows that plant managers are not following federal safety standards. A political campaign worker who sees a candidate accepting illegal contributions. A repentant drug dealer. Such people may be willing to "blow the whistle" and tell their stories to a reporter, but only if they know they will not be identified publicly. Once their names are known, whistleblowers stand a good chance of losing their jobs, or in the case of these involved in illegal drug dealings or organized crime, their lives. Or they may be ordered to undergo punitive and humiliating psychiatric examinations. That's what happened to workers at four federal nuclear weapons facilities after the workers complained about poor safety conditions. One of the four was employed at the Fernald, Ohio, plant that in 1988 was revealed to have a thirty-seven year history of radiation leaks.

Shield laws are important because without them, whistleblowers would be rare, and journalists — and the public — would know a lot less than they do now about public and private crime, corruption, inefficiency, and mismanagement. The laws, incidentally, do not protect reporters and their sources under all circumstances. Reporters found to be hiding knowledge needed to pursue a criminal investigation, for example, may have to choose between protecting a source and going to jail.

Still other media limits could be imposed by the courts. In 1988 a federal appeals court ruled that U.S. copyright law allows public figures to keep writers, historians, and others from quoting from their unpublished letters or diaries. The "expression of an idea, as distinguished from the idea itself, is not considered subject to the public's 'right to know,' " the court concluded. The decision reflected another one from the previous year that prohibited publication of a biography of the reclusive author J. D. Salinger because it included quotations from his letters. Constitutional lawyer Floyd Abrams criticized both rulings as endangering Americans' First Amendment rights.

Furthermore, a 1988 study by the Society of Professional Journalists showed judges at all levels, federal, state, and local, as increasingly willing to hold proceedings behind closed doors and to issue "gag orders," which keep jurors, witnesses, and court employees from discussing cases with reporters. "These restrictions," says Paul Fisher, director of the University of Missouri Freedom of Information Center, "raised judicial censoring power to heights not known in the last half century."

This censorship is not meant solely, or even primarily, to protect men and women involved in criminal cases. Rather, the Association of Trial Lawyers of America (ATLA) reported in the summer of 1989, it is used to keep valuable consumer information secret. As a result of recent judicial orders, says ATLA's president, Bill Wagner, "The truth about lethal fuel systems, exploding lighters, faulty medical devices and procedures, contaminated food, vehicle flipovers, and other life-threatening situations is lost to the public." Paul K. McMasters, chairman of the Society of Professional Journalists' freedom of information committee, calls the new willingness of judges to impose courtroom restraints "anathema to what journalists view as an open society."

Media people also regard as anathema the possibility that the protection of shield laws will be taken away and are equally upset at the prospect of states passing new laws aimed at limiting their ability to conduct Watergate-style investigative reporting. If job applications and ré-sumés are to be kept from the public, wrote the managing editor of one New England newspaper, "people will have absolutely no right to find out anything about people interviewed by city councils or boards of selectmen for such jobs as fire chief, town manager, civic center director or police chief. . . . These people are all trying to get on the public payroll and become employees of the taxpayer." So shouldn't the taxpaying public have the right to know who they are? he demanded. Making secrets out of investigations into charges of unprofessional behavior would, reporters and editors contend, needlessly restrict the public's right to know. And once lawmakers and the courts start imposing limits on the media, who knows where they will stop?

What can news professionals do to avoid limits? In 1988 reporter William Boot offered a succinct suggestion in the *Columbia Journalism Review:* "Don't print, investigate." And, perhaps even more to the point, "If the rumor proves false, debunk it." Not on page 42, either, he might have said. Put the real story up front, where everyone can see it. Invest the accurate, if dull, truth with the same importance and sense of urgency accorded the sensational — and often false — rumor.

Boot had another idea. Why shouldn't journalists, ever eager to put others under the media microscope, to uncover their secrets and compel them to public confession, start to scrutinize their own mistakes and improprieties with the same degree of intensity? "Now is the time," he wrote, "for journalists to come clean." Reporters could well do some confessing of their own, Boot said, and he was willing to suggest the words they might use: "I participated in a cult of personality reporting that trivialized the news. I spread unverified stories, caused unnecessary pain and distorted reality. It was all a mistake and I regret it."

Joanne Jacobs of the San Jose *Mercury News* had a suggestion, too. Reporters ought to act with caution on the 1989 appeals court decision giving them the green light to twist the words of those in the news, making them appear to have said things they may never have dreamed of saying. The day that decision came down was "not a great day for journalism," Jacobs wrote. She compares "faking, fudging, doctoring or hyping quotes" to the new television practice of mixing the dramatic re-creation of events with film of the events themselves. "It's blurring the line between what happened and what could have happened," she says, "between reporting and docudrama. It's lying."

We, as members of the public, can do our own part to help curb media excesses. As Lee Hart, wife of the former senator, wrote a year after seeing her husband's career fall into disarray, it is to please the news-consuming public that media people dig and delve — and sometimes devastate and destroy in the process. "We are all responsible" for what the media do, Lee Hart believes, all of us "who, over the past few years, have developed an increasing, perverse and illegitimate appetite for what ought to be the private business of public people." The private business of private people, too, of course.

9

Secrecy, Security, and the Public Interest

When, in 1988, officials at the U.S. Department of Energy (DOE) announced that radioactive uranium emissions from a nuclear weapons facility in Fernald, Ohio, had contaminated the air and water in its vicinity, the news did not come as much of a surprise to Ken and Lisa Crawford.

In 1979 the Crawfords had rented a farmhouse across the road from the plant — the Feed Materials Production Center, its sign proclaimed. Ken and Lisa assumed the place had something to do with pet foods. In 1984, though, the two began hearing stories about uranium releases, and early the next year their landlord told them that their well was one of three in the neighborhood polluted with the cancer-causing stuff. Ken and Lisa switched to bottled water — and began pressing DOE officials for facts about the seriousness of the contamination. Those officials kept them waiting for nearly four years. At last, on October 14, 1988, they acknowledged that thousands of tons of airborne uranium particles had been released from the deceptively named plant. And thousands of tons had run off into the nearby Great Miami River. Little surprise there for the Crawfords.

What did shock the couple was the admission by the DOE that the releases had begun as far back as 1951, the year the plant opened. People at the company who were responsible for its day-to-day management had known of the problem throughout those thirty-seven years but had said and done nothing about it. Nor had officials of the federal government done anything. For close to four decades government and private industry had cooperated in the cover-up.

Government and industry have participated in other cover-ups to keep the public from finding out about nuclear hazards. In the 1950s the U.S. Army was conducting nuclear weapons tests in the Nevada desert. Ranchers there complained that their sheep were falling sick and dying. Could the deaths have anything to do with radiation released during the testing? Army officials said not, and their denials were confirmed by President Dwight D. Eisenhower. Today we know for sure that the animals' deaths were caused by nuclear fallout. Government and its private nuclear contractors have concealed more dramatic incidents as well. Starting in 1957 and continuing for thirty-one years, a series of accidents occurred at a nuclear weapons plant in Savannah River, South Carolina. Several of the accidents were among the country's most severe, and at least one resulted in widespread contamination. But the public knew nothing of the accidents until Congress raised the alarm in 1988.

Why the long conspiracy of silence? It originated in concern for national security.

As most military professionals see it, our security depends upon the number and quality of our nuclear weapons. Starting at the end of World War II, America sought to protect itself (against, first and foremost, the Soviet Union) by relying upon a theory of nuclear deterrence. According to this theory, the way to keep the Soviets from attacking was to scare them. How? By convincing them that a nuclear attack on their part would be met by a counterattack so overwhelming that it would end, not in Soviet victory, but in Soviet annihilation. To convince the Soviets, the theory continued, the United States had to maintain a huge and ever-growing nuclear arsenal. Any gap in the arsenal would invite Soviet attack — and Soviet domination of the world.

Many who thought this way found it easy to justify a policy of keeping the public ignorant about test site contamination, uranium leaks, and nuclear accidents. If people knew about such problems, the reasoning went, they would want something done to correct them. For instance, they might demand laws requiring emissions-control devices at weapons plants. They might insist that as plants aged and became more radioactive, they be closed down. They might call for the redesign of accident-prone facilities or reduced testing of nuclear weapons. Any of these courses of action could interfere with weapons production.

Such interference would be incompatible, the argument went on, with the demands of national security. If the U.S. arsenal failed to expand on schedule, the entire country, and every person in it, would be at risk. To America's military and military-industrial leaders, the logic was inescapable: the way to protect America was to protect its nuclear arms industry. The way to protect the industry was to keep quiet about its problems. And the way to ensure quiet was to seal the industry off from public scrutiny and clamp a lid of absolute secrecy over it.

So that was what was done in the days just after World War II. In 1946 Congress passed the Atomic Energy Act, which separated nuclear information from all other types of information and required that it be treated differently. Up to then, U.S. law allowed information to be classified as secret if it seemed vital to the national security. But according to Donna Demac of PEN American Center, a group devoted to protecting free-speech rights, the Atomic Energy Act of 1946 "went far beyond earlier regulations by declaring an entire body of knowledge secret." Under the act, anything relating to nuclear research and development was "born classified," meaning it automatically fell into the top-secret category. The secrecy extended, as Ken and Lisa Crawford were to learn nearly half a century later, to all aspects of nuclear knowledge and the nuclear industry, including such public interest concerns as health and safety.

"Somebody should have told us," Lisa said in 1989, her mind on cancer statistics in and around Fernald. Researchers from Johns Hopkins University in Baltimore have found that the death rate from colon cancer there is 21 percent above the national average, while the breast cancer death rate is 31 percent higher than average. The Fernald area is in the top 2 percent of the whole United States in deaths from cancers of the bladder, liver, and lungs. Ken Crawford's father was operated on for cancer, and so was his baby niece. Most of all, Lisa worried about her ten-year-old son. What would his future be? How had his security been served, she wondered, by being forced to breathe and drink uranium? How ironic if he and thousands of others around the country find themselves protected from Soviet nuclear weapons, only to fall victim to America's.

The irony could go further — much further, some Americans believe. In their view, an exaggerated concern for national security is being allowed to override the public interest, not just when it comes to nuclear arms, but in a wide range of areas. Our open, democratic society is in danger of turning into a closed, secretive one, they warn, one in which government makes decisions behind the scenes and acts privately, closed off from public view and shielded from public comment and criticism. And, they add, the change is being made — here's the irony — in the name of protecting our free society from such historically unfree ones as that of the Soviet Union.

People who believe that American democracy may be jeopardized by a growing obsession with secrecy remind us that this country has two distinct traditions: one of public openness and honesty and another of silence and censorship. We've seen examples of both throughout this book. The Zenger trial, the First Amendment, Supreme Court opinions in cases like *Schenck v. U.S.* and *Griswold v. Connecticut,* passage of the Freedom of Information Act of 1966, news reporting on the Watergate affair — all stand as elements of the first tradition. But elements of the second have been deeply entwined among them: colonial licensing laws, the 1798 Sedition Act, censorship before and during the Civil War, the anti–free speech laws of World Wars I and II, and the political repression of the 1950s.

The intertwining of the disparate traditions continued through the 1970s. As the Watergate scandal unfolded, President Nixon refused to give Congress certain documents it had requested. In doing so he invoked "executive privilege," maintaining that presidents have a right, inherent in the Constitution although not specifically spelled out in it, to withhold records of their White House activities. In 1974 the Supreme Court ruled against Nixon, ordering him to hand over the documents. That decision, however, did not put an end to claims of executive privilege. President Ronald Reagan pushed the courts to recognize such claims throughout his eight-year administration, from 1981 to 1989.

The Nixon administration also sought to impose direct censorship upon the nation's press. On June 13, 1971, the *New York Times* began carrying excerpts from a Department of Defense study of the early years of the Vietnam War. As soon as the first installment of the so-called Pentagon Papers appeared, government lawyers went to court to argue that since the study was based on classified material, printing any part of it threatened the national security. The lawyers got a court order halting publication. Lawyers for the *Times* appealed, contending that the real reason the government wanted to keep the Pentagon Papers secret had less to do with security than with the fact that the study was critical of decisions made by U.S. political and military leaders. But it was precisely because those decisions had been flawed that people needed to know about them, lawyers for the *Times* said. Knowing would help Americans understand what mistakes had been made in Vietnam, and understanding might enable them to keep similar mistakes from being made again. The public's First Amendment rights outweighed any consideration of national security in this instance. The Supreme Court agreed and, on June 30, lifted the prior restraint order. The *Times* resumed publication at once.

Yet even as President Nixon demanded censorship and claimed executive privilege, he also took steps to increase openness in government. He changed the federal system of classifying documents, for example, in order to make information more readily available to the press and the public. The next two presidents, Gerald Ford and Jimmy Carter, opened the system up still more. Lawmakers, too, were acting against secrecy. As we saw in Chapter Three, Congress strengthened the FOIA in 1974. Two years later it passed a measure requiring federal agencies to allow the public to attend, and offer comment at, more of their proceedings. Similar "sunshine laws" and freedom of information statutes were enacted by state legislatures, too. The idea of the public's right to know appeared to have become a permanent part of American life.

But as we also saw earlier, new changes in the right to know came in the 1980s. Those changes, all aimed at increasing secrecy, were initiated by President Ronald Reagan and members of his administration. They reflected the administration's conviction that the openness of the 1960s and 1970s — not only in government, but in industry, science, and other areas — had placed the United States in grave danger.

That openness, administration leaders said, was no more than an invitation to America's enemies. All around the country foreign agents were at work, they warned, spying out facts and figures from every available source. They were collecting this bit of information here, that one there, and fitting them together into an enormous "information mosaic." By itself, each fact might be quite harmless, but the completed mosaic would not be in the least harmless. Rather, it would reveal a detailed picture of the country's security and defense systems.

How to keep the mosaic from taking shape? Keep track of information and don't let even the most innocent-seeming scrap leak out. As national security adviser Richard V. Allen explained in 1983, that meant extending controls to "virtually every facet of international activity, including (but not limited to) foreign affairs, defense, intelligence, research and development policy, outer space, international economic and trade policy, and . . . the domains of the Departments of Commerce and Agriculture.''

As part of their overall plan to control information, Reagan and his aides undertook to persuade Congress to weaken the FOIA. The law as it stood was a threat to national security, they argued, since anyone — including foreign agents — could call on it to gain insight into the activities of the Central Intelligence Agency. For several years legislators resisted the White House arguments, but in 1985 they finally agreed to exclude certain CIA files from the provision of the FOIA. The exclusions may or may not be making things more difficult for enemy agents, but the change has definitely cut into Americans' ability to find out about secret — sometimes illegal — CIA operations.

On October 27, 1986, Congress changed the FOIA again. Almost without being aware of it, the lawmakers rendered the law more difficult and more expensive to use. Or so the Fund for Open Information and Accountability, Inc. (FOIA, Inc.) claims. FOIA, Inc. is a public interest group than encourages FOIA use. The 1986 FOIA amendments, says FOIA, Inc., were tacked onto a bill dealing with illegal drugs that Congress was due to consider just before its scheduled fall adjournment. In their keenness to demonstrate their antidrug fervor — and their haste to end the session — members passed the entire bill without taking a good look at the amendments. Passage of the amendments also went virtually unnoticed in the news media. In fact, FOIA, Inc. asserts, an October 18 editorial in the *Washington Post* stated that they had been dropped from the drug bill.

Post editorialists were mistaken. The amendments were in place and did become law. Already they have affected public access to information. In 1987 reporter Scott Armstrong, director of the National Security Archive, told Congress that the act can no longer be used by an individual "who does not have five years, $20,000 to $100,000 for legal fees, and infinite patience." Who might that individual be? A journalist for a local newspaper? A resident of Fernald, Ohio? Someone reading this book? Anyone may need to examine a secret government file. Ask Todd Patterson. As a New Jersey sixth-grader, Todd began writing to foreign embassies, including the Soviet embassy, for a school project. Ever alert for nefarious activity, the FBI began investigating Todd and by 1989, when he was a college freshman, his file had grown to over thirty pages. Todd has been allowed to see only six heavily censored pages of it. It's questionable whether he has the time, money, or patience needed to get a hold of the rest.

Todd Patterson is not the only ordinary citizen to have come under FBI surveillance. Anyone who speaks out against government policies and actions may be investigated. In the 1950s and 1960s, for instance, agents kept files on civil rights activists. Later their focus shifted to anti–Vietnam War protesters. By the 1980s they were investigating men and women protesting against U.S. intervention in Central America.

As we saw in Chapter Five, the Reagan administration considered this intervention — aimed at keeping communism in check — essential to the nation's security. The president had twin aims in Central America: replacing Nicaragua's socialist, pro-Soviet government with one friendly to the United States and helping the pro-American leaders of neighboring El Salvador to withstand a popular left-wing revolution. Millions of dollars' worth of military supplies and equipment were dispatched to El Salvador's government, and U.S. military advisers were sent in, too. Nicaragua's anticommunist rebels were similarly supplied and equipped. Some of this activity had been authorized by Congress, but much, including that engineered by Marine Colonel Oliver North, had not.

Whether or not the U.S. actions in Central America were legal, many Americans disapproved. Intervention there was unwise, they believed, because it could easily lead this country into another Vietnamlike conflict. American involvement in Southeast Asia had begun with military advisers and equipment, too, and with sometimes illegal covert missions. Among the groups protesting U.S. policy in Central America in the early 1980s was the Committee in Support of the People of El Salvador (CISPES).

The Reagan administration's reaction to CISPES and other dissenting groups was to set the FBI on them. Not because group members were breaking any law —

political dissent is entirely legal under the Constitution. But the president and his aides did feel that the threat the groups posed to national security was serious enough to justify strong action. So the FBI began spying on individuals, eventually collecting a total of 4,000 pages of information. Besides that, agents infiltrated the groups themselves, gaining their members' confidence, then sabotaging their work. According to Donna Demac of PEN American Center, former FBI agent Frank Varelli's assignment "included stealing documents and preparing false literature that was then distributed under the CISPES name." The literature was meant to embarrass and discredit the organization. Varelli was also told to "develop a sexual relationship" with one CISPES leader so that he would later be in a position to blackmail her.

Thanks to the FOIA, CISPES and we know about this activity. In 1988, after struggling for several years, lawyers acting on CISPES's behalf got to see 1,300 pages of the FBI's files on the group. The other 2,700 remain buried in secret vaults. Will anyone, given the strict new FOIA rules, ever learn what they say? And about whom? What about domestic spying now and in the future? Will we get to know of it? Should we? Where should the line be drawn between the demands of national security and the public interest, between the concerns of government and the people's hard-won right to know?

Narrowing the FOIA was only part of the Reagan administration's plan to control information. In 1983 the president issued National Security Decision Directive 84

(NSDD 84), requiring federal employees with access to sensitive information to sign an agreement never to reveal any of that information. The lifetime agreements called for employees, both past and present, to submit book manuscripts and other materials to the agency by which they were employed for prepublication review. The agency's right to censor the material, classified or not, was to be absolute.

Reaction to NSDD 84 was swift. Conservative columnist William Safire, a Reagan supporter, called the directive "a rape of principle" and said that the day the president signed it would "live in constitutional infamy." Free-press advocate Donna Demac wrote that the agreements were "a blatant violation of the free speech rights of a large number of American citizens." Mark Lynch, an attorney with the American Civil Liberties Union (ACLU), predicted that they would "make it extremely difficult for any former official to function as a newspaper columnist, radio or TV commentator, or to participate in political debate, since many of their writings will be subject to a time delay while being cleared." A congressional outcry forced the administration to issue a new, supposedly less restrictive rule concerning prepublication review in 1984. However, says the General Accounting Office (GAO), after the second rule went into effect more material, not less, came under review.

The controversial agreements apply to fiction as well as nonfiction. In 1987 ex-CIA employee Bob Andrews wrote a spy novel called *Center Game*. When his former bosses read the manuscript, they called Andrews into their office and demanded alterations and deletions on the spot. ''You don't leave this room until you change this,'' Andrews reports they told him.

Directives like the one that allowed the CIA to demand — and get — changes in Andrews's thriller had become a frequently used presidential policy-making tool by the beginning of the 1990s. Originally known as National Security Action Memorandums (NSAMs), the orders were made possible under the National Security Act of 1947. They are automatically classified: each one is written, signed, and issued in secret, its contents known only to the president and a few advisers with top-security clearance. Whole or partial declassification may come later.

The nature of NSDDs has changed since 1947. At first they consisted of general policy outlines. But, says reporter Eve Pell, ''Over the years these directives have evolved from broad statements to specific decrees that . . . can . . . authorize the commitment of federal resources.'' It certainly is easier for a chief executive to make commitments that way than through the often tedious process of negotiating them through a reluctant Congress. After the United States became involved in the fighting in Vietnam, for example, it occurred to President Lyndon Johnson that he could bring the war to a quick end by sending American troops into neighboring Laos to ''clean out'' communists there. He wasn't sure, however, that he could get Congress to support such an invasion, so he signed an NSAM giving himself the authority to order it. Simple.

Unfortunately, events did not turn out as Johnson expected. Going into Laos not only didn't end the war, it widened and prolonged it. Perhaps invading Laos wasn't such a great idea after all. Perhaps if Congress had known about the plan and had had a chance to examine and debate it, the country would have been better off.

But Congress can't examine and debate if presidents replace government by legislation with government by secret decree. And, almost entirely unknown to Americans, that is just what they seem to be doing. During his eight years in office, President Reagan issued about three hundred NSDDs. Their subject matter ranged from nuclear weapons policy to Central America; from the handling of classified information to civil defense plans; from arms sales to foreign aid; from meetings with Soviet leaders to the space shuttle. According to the *Washington Post,* an NSDD led the National Aeronautics and Space Administration (NASA) to rush the launch of the shuttle *Challenger* in January 1986. The spaceship, with its leaky, poorly designed seals, was launched on a day when the air temperature was lower than the minimum needed for safety. *Challenger* exploded, killing all seven people on board.

What other unknown dictates may be out there waiting to change our lives in years to come? "Is there a plan to void the Constitution in the event of large anti-Administration demonstrations?" Pell asked in 1989.

"Are old military bases being considered as detention camps for political dissidents?" She continued, "During the past eight years, press reports have suggested that such actions were authorized by a still-secret NSDD." We may never know whether the reports are true. Only about fifty of Reagan's NSDDs had been even partially declassified by 1990. By that time, President George Bush had begun issuing his own. His first directive changed their appellation to National Security Directives (NSDs).

Another information control step of the 1980s reversed the policy followed by Nixon, Ford, and Carter of relaxing the security classification system. Under a 1982 executive order federal officials got broader-than-ever powers to classify information. Executive orders, incidentally, differ from NSDDs and must be counted separately from them.

The 1982 order was another part of the plan to keep the dangerous information mosaic from taking shape. "Instead of having to demonstrate 'identifiable damage' to national security, today officials need only point out that 'disclosure reasonably could be expected to cause damage to the national security.' " John Shattuck and Muriel Morisey Spence wrote in *Technology Review* magazine. Shattuck is vice president for government, community, and public affairs at Harvard University, and Spence is director of policy analysis at Harvard's Office of Government, Community, and Public Affairs. What the order amounted to was, When in doubt, classify. And that's what government officials did. According to the Information Security Oversight Office, the number of separate pieces of information stamped secret rose from 16 million in 1980 to 23 million three years later. The 1982 order also did away with an earlier requirement limiting the length of time that material can remain classified and permitted the classifying of information even after it has been made available to the public. This latter provision, Shattuck and Spence point out, could have the effect of stifling scientific research. People may be less willing to make "long-term intellectual investments" in fields "likely to be classified at a later date."

Four years later the administration tried to control unclassified facts and figures as well. Under a directive issued in October 1986, restrictions were placed on exchanging unclassified material via computer in areas relating to such "government interests" as "economic, human, financial, industrial, agricultural, technological, and law enforcement information." The directive "prompted fears that U.S. intelligence agencies would monitor virtually all . . . information exchanges," say Shattuck and Spence, and was withdrawn under congressional pressure in March 1987. Even so, the two from Harvard add, the restrictions limit the sharing of information with people who are not American citizens.

The effort to keep information out of foreign hands represented another change for the United States. Until the 1980s this country generally acted on the assumption that scientific and technical advances are most likely to take place in a world in which knowledge is shared freely. The Soviet Union, by contrast, relied upon secrecy in its effort to forge ahead scientifically. The Soviet reliance was misplaced, Shattuck and Spence conclude, and their conclusion is backed by evidence from such groups as the American Physical Society. The society cites, in particular, "well-known Soviet lags in solid-state electronics and biology."

From now on the United States may be the nation that lags behind. In 1985 the U.S. Department of Defense placed restrictions on foreign participation in a conference on photo-optical research. (The foreigners in this instance were Canadians.) DOD officials didn't want information about research in laser weaponry — an application of photo-optic theory — leaving the country. Twelve leading scientific organizations, including the American Association for the Advancement of Science and the American Chemical Society, protested the restrictions, but to no avail. The next year DOD officials took six weeks to review papers scheduled for delivery at a nuclear physics conference. On the very morning the conference was to begin, thirteen authors were told they could not make their presentations.

In a further move aimed at limiting the opportunities of foreigners to keep up with U.S. science and technology, the FBI attempted in 1986 to enlist the nation's librarians as part-time agents. Staffers at a number of libraries — twenty-one in the New York City area alone, and others from Florida to Utah, and Ohio to California — were asked to keep an eye out for "hostile intelligence people." The FBI wanted the librarians to keep track of the materials such people requested and borrowed and to report back to the agency. Library workers, conscious of their commitment to what one called "the cultivation of an informed citizenry," refused. Their refusal prompted the FBI to conduct background checks on the librarians themselves.

Information was not the only commodity the Reagan administration was unwilling to share with the world. Limits were also placed on international sales of manufactured items like computers. The reason: high-tech goods could be used in the making of weapons that might one day be directed against the United States or its allies.

But is "might" reason enough for tightening controls on exports? Shattuck and Spence think not. One victim of controls, they caution, "is likely to be U.S. security itself," since "the long-term technological progress on which it depends [will be] impeded." Yet another irony: the federal government threatens to weaken the national defense in the act of "strengthening" it.

Critics point to other drawbacks of measures to control information, for example, the financial costs. According to a 1987 report by the National Academy of Sciences, "controls on the export of manufactured goods and information cost the U.S. economy 188,000 jobs and $9 billion a year." And the restrictions may affect Americans' quality of life in other ways. Many of the consumer products with which we are familiar today — like nonstick Teflon coating for cookware — resulted from technology originally developed for the U.S. space exploration program. If science and industry are no longer permitted to share such technology, the public will end up paying the price.

There may be other prices to pay, the critics warn, since the 1980s movement toward secrecy did not stop with matters of national security. Remember that Reagan had been in office just over a week when he suspended rules changes that would have made more information available to buyers of new cars and to nursing home patients. During the 1980s Americans found it harder and harder to get the facts about other consumer issues, such as federal meat and poultry inspection policies and environmental cleanup programs.

The administration also took some of the light out of the sunshine laws of the 1970s. For instance, the Federal Communications Commission announced in 1986 that it would no longer publish the full texts of proposed changes in rules for the broadcasting industry. Summaries of these proposals are all that now appear in the *Federal Register*. The policy makes it harder for the public to comment on the proposals or to question them. The FCC defended its new way of doing things by saying that it reduced paperwork and saved money at the federal level.

No doubt a great many Americans would say that saving money and cutting down on paperwork were reasons enough to substitute summaries for full texts. Who, besides the broadcasters themselves, needs to know the details of the proposed regulations of the industry?

But it's not really that simple, others argue. FCC rules are more than just an arcane set of instructions for industry insiders. They affect everything that goes out over the airwaves, including news and reenactments of the news, business and consumer information, docudramas with a political point of view — the lot. Federal rules affect the on-air balance of opinion, too. The commissioners' 1987 decision to scrap the fairness doctrine was a momentous one. Before that date station owners were required to present a variety of opinions on controversial issues. Afterward owners were free to broadcast their own views exclusively. The change, critics believe, will have the effect of limiting popular debate and discussion. Is saving money and cutting down on government paperwork worth that? Are those goals, worthy though they may be, more important than seeing to it that the public is fully informed?

Once again, the way people answer that question will depend upon where they decide to draw the line between the needs of government and those of the governed.

10

Information and Misinformation

What exactly happened in and around Tiananmen Square in Beijing, China, on June 4, 1989? Everyone knows what happened there in the weeks leading up to that date. Chinese from all walks of life — students, teachers, workers, farmers, housewives, children, and the elderly — had gathered to voice their demands for democracy and individual rights. For a while it seemed as if those demands might be met. The world was watching, thanks largely to American TV, and many in China's government were loathe to be seen using violence against their own people. Some officials genuinely sympathized with the demonstrators. Other advocated taking a hard line and sending in the army to crush the protest.

The way some tell it, it was the hard-liners who won the internal power struggle. In the first days of June, they say, officials sympathetic to the students were removed from their government posts. Then, during the night of June 3–4, army tanks rolled into the streets surrounding the square. Soldiers of the People's Liberation Army beat up students and workers and aimed their assault rifles at young and old alike. Hundreds of civilians died, witnesses claim, and so did a hundred-odd soldiers. Afterward, the scars of battle were plainly visible — bloodstains on streets and sidewalks, great gouges in curbs and steps where heavy caterpillar-tread vehicles had mounted them, and bullet-ridden building façades.

Others tell the story differently. "It never happened that soldiers fired directly at the people," one Chinese general insisted at a mid-June press conference. Questioned by reporters, including members of the U.S. press, about the bullet holes and the tank tracks, other officials were equally bland. Staring directly at the marks, one official repeated the same refrain: "It never happened. It never happened." What had happened in Tiananmen Square on June 4, the government said, was that crowds viciously attacked a contingent of Liberation Army soldiers, killing about a hundred of them. Perhaps as many as a hundred civilians also died, the victims of their fellow rioters.

Chinese officialdom offered more than mere words to back its claims. The state-run media carried pictures of one dead soldier and repeated, over and over and over, the government's tale of the brutal fashion in which he had been slain. Interviews with the soldier's parents and brother were broadcast and rebroadcast. Again and again the three expressed outrage at the "thugs" their leaders had assured them were responsible for his death. Witnesses who on June 5 or 6 had spoken of killings and beatings by the People's Army disappeared, their places on television and in newspaper columns taken by men and women eager to confirm the government's version of events. There were few to contradict this second group of "witnesses," and none who dared speak publicly. By July China was quiet once more, any movement toward democracy at a standstill, for the time anyway. The nation's propaganda machine had done its job.

Could a propaganda effort so blatant work in the United States? No. The technique of the Big Lie, the official untruth repeated over and over until it assumes a semblance of reality, can be effective in a totalitarian state, but not in a society with a right to know and a free and open press. In America, information management is far more subtle.

Subtle . . . but it's there. Who does the managing? Government, of course, as well as people in business and industry, members of political parties and consumer groups, professionals, the clergy, men and women in the news business — anyone, in short, with access to the media and a point of view to get across. As an example of one way news and information are managed, consider the fanfare with which the B-2 bomber was unveiled before the U.S. public.

The idea of the B-2 was cooked up by the Department of Defense under President Jimmy Carter, adopted by the Reagan administration, and later espoused by President George Bush. Also known as the Stealth, because it is supposed to be able to slip through radar undetected, the

B-2 would be used in the aftermath of a nuclear war. (That is, as critics would say, if there is an aftermath.) When research on the bomber began, the DOD decreed that everything about it would be kept secret. Everything. Its exact cost to the taxpaying public was classified. So were the schedules of its design, production, and testing stages. Even the plane's precise role after a nuclear war was left unspecified.

The secrecy that surrounded the B-2 was essential, officials thought, to national security. But by the time the project was a decade old, they realized that in terms of getting Congress and the public to agree that the bomber was necessary — and worth paying for — secrecy had its drawbacks. That's why DOD took the wraps off Stealth in July 1989 and invited the press to be present at what *Time* magazine called history's most visible first flight. Department officials hoped to create enthusiasm among reporters, enthusiasm that the media would then transmit to the rest of the nation.

To a degree they succeeded. Several reporters, moving beyond fact into the realm of opinion, described the test flight as "beautiful" or "perfect." The *New York Times* gave Deputy Secretary of Defense Donald J. Atwood space on its op-ed page (opposite the page with editorials and letters to the editor) for a piece entitled "Why Stealth Makes Sense." Atwood described "this revolutionary aircraft . . . virtually invisible to radar . . . national security costs of not going ahead. . . ." But DOD's exercise in public relations, or PR, was not an unqualified success. Some press reports reminded people that the much-publicized flight showed only that the bomber could get off the ground, not that it was invisible to radar. Days after the test Congress disappointed DOD and the administration by cutting the funding for Stealth.

That setback didn't mark the end of Stealth, though, nor of DOD propaganda meant to encourage congressional and public support for the project. And Stealth propaganda is only part of the department's PR effort. DOD, in turn, is just one of the thousands of agencies at all levels of government that routinely try to convey information in order to accomplish specific goals. Remember how ABC-TV's impatience to get on the air with a special about illegal drugs forced state and federal law agencies to carry out a raid ahead of schedule? The agencies later suggested that the network had acted irresponsibly. But they were the ones who had compromised their operation in the first place by inviting reporters to film it. Why the invitation? It was part of an effort to win public appreciation and support for the agencies' activities in the war against drugs.

Individuals in government are as eager for good public relations as the agencies that employ them. The eagerness is particularly pronounced at election time, causing political analysts to observe that modern campaigns have degenerated into little more than exercises in managing people's perceptions of reality. Style, not substance, is what's emphasized. Candidates may not be able to answer reporters' questions about what might be done to improve the quality of education, but they have no trouble grinning at a roomful of kindergartners as the cameras whir away. They may not have specific recommendations about joblessness or farmers who cannot afford to stay on their land, but they'll put in an appearance at busy factory gates and wave cheerfully from atop a tractor. Presidential nominating conventions are no longer held for their original purpose of selecting candidates; they are staged-for-TV extravaganzas. For its 1988 convention the Democratic party chose a hall so small that many participants could not squeeze inside. It was just the right size to look good on television, though.

Even when the election is over, the victor's personal PR campaign continues. President Reagan was a master of such campaigning. Each move he made was meticulously orchestrated. During his public appearances every route, right down to his path across a room, was mapped out in advance. Tapes marked exactly where he was to stand at each moment. Nor did Reagan ever face the press unrehearsed. The questions that were likely to be asked were discussed with advisers ahead of time, a practice that irritated reporters looking for spontaneity. President George Bush, like such other chief executives as Gerald Ford, Lyndon Johnson, and John Kennedy, delighted reporters by talking with them more frequently and informally.

Still, Bush was not above using reporters, and with the help of aides he proved himself an able manipulator of the media. Early in 1989 the White House organized a marathon twelve-hour "photo opportunity" session with *Time*. The result was six full-color pages in the May 22 issue: the president at his desk, with an aide, signing an autograph, getting a CIA briefing, headed for a party. "A Busy Thursday," *Time* called the spread, and the day "a tough twelve hours." Probably it was. But what was Bush's priority during those hours? Governing the nation? Or being seen governing the nation?

Presidents are not the only ones on the lookout for favorable coverage, and photo opportunities are a media mainstay, as a glance at the evening news or the daily paper demonstrates. A senator chats with constituents; the mayor crowns a beauty queen; a bank officer opens a new branch; environmentalists dedicate a recycling center; a police chief inspects the city lockup; the president of the Parent-Teachers Association passes out cookies at a classroom party — "news" of this type fills minute after minute, page after page. Such "fluff pieces" may be innocent enough, but other efforts to garner good publicity are not.

During the 1980s, for example, officials at the federal Environmental Protection Agency (EPA) talked a lot about their commitment to getting industry to stop polluting the country's land, air, and water. The talk was good PR; it was what Americans wanted to hear. But agency officials didn't stop at PR. They destroyed or concealed documents showing not only that they had done virtually nothing to clean up the environment, but also that many of them had close business and personal relationships with executives at the very companies doing the worst polluting. President Reagan tried to assist in the cover-up by claiming that documents not already shredded were protected by executive privilege. However, enough papers did come to light to create a mighty scandal that cost several EPA high officials their jobs. On the state level Maine's EPA kept quiet about the sewage that was washing up at public beaches in the late 1980s. Why? One editorial writer hinted at an answer. "Who would want to come to Maine in the summer to swim in the same bacteria they could find in New Jersey? Why make the trip?" Tourism is among the state's most lucrative industries, as state officials are aware. But surely tourists — and Mainers — are entitled to know whether the waters they're swimming in are clean.

Pollution isn't the only problem that "doesn't exist" when it is not reported. In her book *The Big Chill,* Eve Pell wrote about cutbacks by the federal government in the 1980s in the collecting and reporting of statistics in a variety of areas, including "regional poverty and health, unemployment, and agriculture." The cuts were initiated as a money-saving measure, Pell conceded, but they had the side effect of obscuring the growth of joblessness, poverty, and homelessness. That obfuscation benefited a White House that was proud of its record on the economy. Business, in bad shape when Reagan took office in 1981, appeared to most Americans to be doing much better eight years later. But was the economy really healthy? Or were people just not hearing all the facts?

Concealing or disguising facts is bad enough, but information management sometimes crosses the line into outright lying. In May 1989 Dr. James E. Hansen, a NASA expert on climate changes, was scheduled to present a written report to Congress and to testify orally before a Senate subcommittee on the relationship between pollution and global warming. The day before the report and his testimony were due, Americans learned that Hansen's report differed considerably from what he would say to the subcommittee.

Hansen is convinced that global warming presents a real danger to life on earth. According to him and others, the burning of fossil fuels like oil, wood, and coal is resulting in a buildup of carbon dioxide and other gases in our atmosphere. The gases trap heat just the way a greenhouse does. This so-called greenhouse effect, Hansen wrote, is likely to mean severe droughts and terrible storms, weather changes that threaten to put stresses — possibly unbearable ones — on living organisms.

As a matter of routine, Hansen's report was sent to the White House Office of Management and the Budget (OMB) for review. Under a 1980 law OMB checks all written matter submitted to the Government Printing Office (GPO) for publication. In theory that gives the executive branch a chance to filter out unnecessary paperwork, thereby saving money. But as a practical matter, it means that OMB — and ultimately the White House — enjoys censorship powers.

In Hansen's case, as in others, those powers were put

to work. OMB refused to allow the GPO to print the report in its original form; the wording was changed to make the threatened greenhouse effect seem less likely than the report's author believes it to be. The changes angered Hansen. "It distresses me that they put words in my mouth; they even put it in the first person," he told reporters. He tried to "negotiate" with OMB censors, he added, but "they refused to change." The reason for their stubbornness, said one senator, was that OMB and the Bush administration did not want Hansen's report to alarm Congress and the public and start them pushing for a proposed international treaty aimed at reducing pollution in the upper air. Neither the senator nor Hansen regarded that as sufficient reason for censorship. "I should be allowed to say what is my scientific position," Hansen protested. "I can understand changing policy, but not science."

OMB officials, of course, wouldn't call what they did changing science. From their point of view, they were putting a "positive spin" on the facts. Their critics might say they had been spreading "disinformation."

Disinformation is a frequently used tool of totalitarian governments. It was a disinformation campaign that the leaders of the People's Republic of China engaged in after the battle at Tiananmen Square. The Soviet Union's use of disinformation — *dezinformatsiya* — has been notorious.

Disinformation has been used as a political and governmental tool in the United States, as well, astonishing as that may seem. The federal government, aided and abetted by private industry, spent years spreading disinformation in the area of Nevada's atom bomb testing range; in Fernald, Ohio; and at other places contaminated by nuclear emissions and wastes, for example. It wasn't just a matter of keeping quiet about the deadly pollution at those sites. Spokespersons lied about it intentionally and directly, offering one assurance after another that no problem existed. They assumed that Americans' sense of patriotism and their trust in government would lull them into accepting the falsehoods.

The U.S. government also employs disinformation on the international level. One particularly controversial use of it occurred in 1986. The campaign began with an article that appeared in the *Wall Street Journal* on August 25. The *Journal* article stated that according to unidentified White House officials, intelligence sources had evidence that the North African nation of Libya was about to begin a new round of terrorist activity against the United States. Since Libya had supported terrorism in the past, the report seemed believable. The same sources, the *Journal* went on, indicated that this country was prepared to attack Libya as soon as the terrorism got under way. That part of the story, too, sounded convincing. The previous April, U.S. warplanes had bombed two Libyan cities in retaliation for earlier terrorist attacks against American targets. When questioned about the intelligence reports, White House staffers, still unnamed, corroborated them.

The reports were lies. On October 2 the *Washington Post* revealed that contrary to the White House claim, there was no evidence that Libya was still bankrolling terrorism. The administration's apparent motive in putting forth the story was to frighten Libyan leaders out of even considering future support for terrorists. Another motive may have been to stir up anti-Libya sentiment at home and to prod Americans into demanding a second military raid. Not everyone found these motives acceptable. State Department spokesman Bernard Kalb, formerly of CBS news, resigned after learning he had been forced into partnership in the scheme. Kalb quit his job, columnist William Safire wrote, "to make the point that nobody who speaks for the United States can tolerate official lying."

The White House conveyed its disinformation about Libya to the *Wall Street Journal* through a process known as leaking. Although information leaks are usually thought of as coming from disgruntled employees, those who disagree with a policy, whistleblowers, and the like, that is generally not the case, says *New York Times* reporter Richard Halloran. "Contrary to the widely held perception," he wrote, " 'leaking' is not solely or even largely the province of the dissident. Rather, it is a political instrument wielded almost daily by senior officials within the administration."

Why would any government official deliberately let slip confidential, even classified, information? Halloran mentioned several reasons: "to influence a decision, to promote policy, to persuade Congress, and to signal foreign governments.'' Certainly the 1986 leak to the *Journal* was intended to send a strong signal to Libya. The evidence also suggests that leaks do amount to a form of internal communication, ''oil in the machinery of government,'' Halloran called them. The ''oil'' lubricates at the highest levels. ''A presidential aide, afraid to confront the president directly with bad news, gets his message across through the press. A Cabinet officer, unable to get [access to the president] . . . leaks a memo that will land on the president's desk in the morning newspaper.''

Even the FBI, despite its carefully tailored reputation as a bastion of discretion, plays the leaking game. During the days of the civil rights movement the agency gave out damaging information, much of it false, about the movement's charismatic leader, Martin Luther King, Jr. The FBI's director, J. Edgar Hoover, thought, or said he thought, that King was a communist, and possibly subversive into the bargain. Acting on Hoover's orders, and with the approval of President John Kennedy and his brother, U.S. Attorney General Robert Kennedy, agents placed King under surveillance, tailing him around the country, tapping his telephone, and planting listening devices in his hotel rooms. Despite a total lack of evidence, Hoover and others in the FBI continually fanned rumors linking King to communism. They also leaked stories about his purported illicit relationships with women.

Decades later the FBI still seemed apt to leak information when doing so suited its purposes. In 1989 the media got wind of FBI suspicions about a man named Felix S. Bloch, a U.S. career diplomat and the second highest officer at the U.S. embassy in Vienna, Austria. Word was that the FBI suspected Bloch of spying for the Soviet Union or one of the communist nations of Eastern Europe but lacked the evidence needed for an arrest. Hearing that, the media took off in hot pursuit, surrounding Bloch's home and dogging him whenever he left it. According to some observers, the unofficial surveillance was exactly what the FBI wanted; if nothing else, the media pressure would keep Bloch from evading his official watchers and slipping out of the country, as had happened in the past. With luck, it might rattle him, perhaps enough to induce a confession. The FBI denied any such motives, protesting rather that the intense coverage had hindered its investigation. Nevertheless, many media analysts remained convinced that the leaks were deliberate, a way to safeguard what the agency saw as the national security.

That's interesting, because government officials are usually quick to portray leaks as seriously endangering that security. Maybe they believe what they say. They certainly act as if they do. President Reagan issued NSDD 84, the directive that made federal employees above a certain security clearance subject to lifelong censorship, after a series of disclosures shed unwanted light on some of his global plans and strategies. "I've had it up to my keister with these leaks," Reagan declared angrily at the time. He was not the first chief executive to react that way. George Washington became furious in 1795 when a senator leaked to a Philadelphia newspaper secret details about a treaty with France. So perturbed was Richard Nixon by leaks that he tried to plug them by illegally tapping the telephones of federal employees suspected of talking out of turn. In a play on words, the agents assigned to do the job were dubbed ''plumbers.''

In point of fact, though, say Richard Halloran and others, leaks rarely damage national security. However, the perception that leaks are damaging — the official perception of most government officials and one unquestioningly accepted by a great percentage of the U.S. public — may be very damaging indeed.

How so? The idea that leaks threaten national security makes it relatively simple for government to override the First Amendment and the concept of the right to know and to impose rules of censorship. People like Donna Demac of PEN American Center consider NSDD 84 one example of such a rule, and the 1982 executive order that expanded the federal classification system another. The 1982 order permits federal employees to put a Top Secret stamp on documents almost at will, and that, the critics say, does far more to protect those employees personally and professionally than to protect the national security. Automatic classification allows government to operate behind the scenes and secures America's elected and appointed leaders against public scrutiny and criticism. ''With so much technically secret,'' say *New York Times* lawyers James Goodale and Lawrence Martin, "no one knows what is truly secret. Officials come to see the stamp as a political tool that allows them to keep secret what would hurt them and to leak what they want publicized.

And a good thing, too! many Americans in and out of government would say. People need to protect themselves from the media. They need to protect themselves personally from intrusive, tell-all reporters, from men and women who do not hesitate to stake out a politician's home, analyze a Supreme Court nominee's video rentals, or paw through someone's garbage. They need to protect themselves professionally from media people who are free to misquote them without fear of a libel suit and to headline false charges against them with no more than a small-print retraction by way of apology. Most of all, though, people need to protect themselves politically against a press that is itself severely politically biased.

Biased in what way? Toward the left, millions of Americans would say. Toward liberalism and away from conservatism; toward Democrats and away from Republicans; toward an overly strong regard for individual liberties and civil rights and away from a concern for government and its rightful authority; toward world peace and away from military preparedness; toward internationalism and away from patriotism — the list could go on indefinitely. And the press bias is all the more dangerous, say members of such conservative watchdog organizations as Accuracy In Media (AIM), because the media are so overwhelmingly rich and powerful, so influential, and, above all, so alike. In fact, groups like AIM tend to talk of the media as if they were a single, monolithic entity — an "it" rather than a "they": the media *is* full of liberal propaganda; the media *is* anti-American.

The idea that men and women in the news and information business are suspect — perhaps even dangerous — is nothing new. It was almost exactly three hundred years ago that Boston officials shut down the first newspaper published in the colonies for taking an anti-government stand. A half century later, John Peter Zenger was put on trial for printing criticism of New York's governor. The Sedition Act of 1798 was passed in part to halt press criticism of President John Adams and his political friends. Abolitionist materials were seen as a threat to stability in the South in the years before the Civil War, and after the war began, President Lincoln took strong measures against what he saw as anti-Union publications. During World War I the assumption that disloyal Americans would use the media to undermine the war effort led to strict censorship laws. Similar assumptions led to similar results when the United States entered World War II. In the 1950s left-wing subversives and would-be traitors were presumed to be lurking throughout the media, disseminating their dangerous ideas in books, newspapers, magazines, and journals; broadcasting them over radio and television; and sneaking them into films and documentaries. Repression followed.

Today most Americans would agree that the presump-

tions of the 1950s were unfounded. Most would also say
that abolitionist writings, inflammatory as they may have
appeared to southern slave holders 150 years ago, were
morally correct. And who would call it unpatriotic or
un-American to criticize a president? Opinion as to the
need for wartime censorship might be more divided. As
the Supreme Court suggested in its decision in the case of
Schenck v. U.S., the normal standards do not necessarily
apply in times of "clear and present danger." Surely
Lincoln was right to keep news of Union troop movements out of the press. What about his orders to close
down newspapers that simply expressed pro-Confederate
opinions, though? And what about the type of censorship
measures imposed during World Wars I and II? To many
they seem harder to justify.

If, with the benefit of hindsight, we can dismiss as
nonthreatening so many past charges of the press's anti-
Americanism and lack of patriotism, what of similar
charges today? Are they equally unwarranted? Are the
media really as uniformly and dangerously liberal as
groups like AIM say?

Certainly it is not the case that conservative opinion and
analysis are not represented in the press. Newspapers com-
monly accused of too much liberalism — the *New York
Times,* for instance, or the *Washington Post* — have plenty
of competition from the *Wall Street Journal* and, on a more
popular level, *USA Today.* So-called liberal papers have
their own conservative columnists, as well. William Safire
writes regularly for the *Times,* for example, and is nation-

ally syndicated. The *Times* and other papers also provide op-ed space for varying points of view and print letters to the editor from a number of sources.

The same spectrum of opinion can be found in the other media. A liberal magazine like *The Nation* is counterbalanced by the right-wing *National Review*. Broadcasting has its conservatives as well. On commercial radio, Paul Harvey provides one well-known example, and on public radio, Zbigniew Brzezinski. Brzezinski served as national security adviser in the Carter administration and is generally suspicious of Soviet motives and intentions in world affairs.

Commercial television, too, makes room for conservative opinion. In planning news programs and talk shows, producers are careful to strike a balance — to counter the liberal with the conservative. And bear in mind that in the United States, "liberal" is most often equated with "Democratic," rather than with anything resembling Western European liberalism or socialism. "Conservative," by contrast, is associated not so much with mainstream Republicanism as with the more radical right wing, as exemplified by a publication like the *National Review*. It is also noteworthy that commercial TV hosts may be less likely to balance conservative points of view with liberal ones. A 1989 analysis of ABC's popular "Nightline" with Ted Koppel showed the guest list leaning strongly to "white male representatives of powerful institutions," people like secretaries and assistant secretaries of state in the Nixon and Reagan administrations, and the Reverend Jerry Falwell, founder of the religiously conservative Moral Majority. The analysis of 865 "Nightline" transcripts was conducted by a group called Fairness and Accuracy in Reporting (FAIR).

Even public television, frequently singled out as being left-leaning, airs such conservative fare as "The Mc-Laughlin Group," "Firing Line," and "One on One." Jeff Cohen, director of FAIR, points out that all three programs are hosted by *National Review* editors. In addition, Cohen says, PBS-TV regularly broadcasts three business programs, but not one devoted to consumer interests. Furthermore, as public funding for PBS has dried up, the system has turned to corporate sources of revenue. Some charge that the change has affected the content of programs. When a private medical insurance company like Blue Cross-Blue Shield underwrites the costs of a program on the current health-care situation in the United States, for example, the result is certain to be a rosier picture than if the program had been paid for by a consumer group or from public donations.

In fact, many critics agree, the media are far more conservative than organizations like AIM are willing to admit. That conservatism shows itself, not so much in the strictly political sense as in moral, social, and economic views.

We've seen examples of such conservatism throughout this book. We've seen, for instance, how business and advertising pressures shape the news and information we get — or don't get. And how the media tend to focus on the personal and trivial — a candidate's love life, a dramatic drug bust — while largely ignoring serious and complex topics like the specifics of how the candidate would go about cleaning up the environment or ways to solve the nation's drug problem. We've seen how facts are distorted in docudramas and how the media are content to cooperate in noncontroversial PR campaigns, to run a flattering, easy-to-write spread on a day in the life of a president, or to print and broadcast puffery about local businesses, law enforcement agencies, and other establishment institutions. We've seen how the media are vulnerable to the technique of government-by-leak and how they have helped smear the reputation of a Dr. King or a Felix Bloch. We've seen how often the media meekly accept the "official version" of events. People in the media didn't question the army's assertion that nuclear fallout was not a problem in Nevada in the 1950s. They left that task to private citizens. Local media covered the Fernald, Ohio, radiation story starting in 1984, but such "liberal" and "unpatriotic" publications as the *New York Times* and the *Nation* didn't pick the story up until public pressure forced DOE officials to admit the facts four years later.

Does all this mean that the media in this country are no more than a tool of the political, economic, industrial, and social establishment? No. Publishing and broadcasting still have their individual heroes and heroines: the journalists who uncovered the Watergate affair; the former reporter whose resignation helped call attention to an ugly disinformation campaign; editors and producers who quit their jobs rather than submit to coercion from business interests. America does have a free and independent press, and Americans do enjoy the right to know. But it's important to remember that freedom of speech and of the press and the right to know and to be informed have not always been part of the American intellectual and political landscape. And unless we take care to guard those rights and freedoms — guard them against trivialization, against the techniques of advertising and public relations, against social, political, and economic forces, against national and international corporate trends, and against much more besides — they may not remain ours.

11

Another Quake, Another Time

This book began with the story of one earthquake. It ends with the story of another.

On December 7, 1988, a quake hit the Soviet Republic of Armenia, destroying one third of the country in an instant. In what had been the city of Leninakan, population 275,000, not a single school or hospital remained standing. No one is sure how many died in the disaster. In the confusion, estimates fluctuated wildly, and even seven months later the final count ranged from 25,000 to 100,000. An estimated 120,000 others were injured, and as many as half a million were left homeless.

Soviet President Mikhail Gorbachev was in New York City when he heard the news. Immediately he canceled his plans for the day — plans that had included a meeting with President Reagan — to fly home to Moscow and on to the scene of the tragedy. Also converging on the scene were reporters — reporters from local papers, from the Soviet press and television, from the United States, from Spain, France, England, and dozens of other places. For this Soviet earthquake was different from ones past. This

ANOTHER QUAKE, ANOTHER TIME　　　151

earthquake the Soviets were talking about and letting others talk about. The talk was part of a new Soviet policy known as *glasnost,* a Russian word that signifies "openness."

Glasnost meant more than just talking about the quake. Soviet officials were also admitting to mistakes that had allowed the toll of death and injury to climb so high. Building construction in cities like Leninakan — construction designed and carried out by government functionaries — was cheap and shoddy, the officials said. That was why so many buildings had collapsed in the shock, crushing their occupants. Initial rescue efforts, again the work of the public authorities, had been so poorly planned and coordinated that thousands of victims had died needlessly. Such admissions would have been unthinkable in the past. Always before, the Soviet government, like that of the People's Republic of China, had tried to conceal disasters, natural or manmade, and had made every effort to cover up its mistakes. Over the years Soviet officials kept silent about earthquakes that killed hundreds of thousands, and as recently as 1986 they hushed up the facts about an accident at a nuclear power plant in the town of Chernobyl. But within just three years of the Chernobyl disaster, glasnost had turned things around for the people of the Soviet Union.

The results must have amazed them. Along with the reporters who arrived in Armenia in mid-December came Julia V. Taft, director of the U.S. government disaster relief agency. She was accompanied by half a dozen trauma physicians and search teams. Paramedics flew in from Florida, Virginia, and elsewhere, bringing with them hundreds of tents, blankets, tools, and pieces of rescue equipment. American food and drug companies donated millions of dollars' worth of their products. Blood supplies arrived from Cuba, and canned beef from Argentina. England, the Scandinavian countries, Japan, even the violence-torn nations of the Middle East — Israel among them — offered aid. Soviet-Israeli relations have been icy over the years, because of Russia's anti-Semitic tradition and because of Soviet support for the Arab nations. But the bad feelings seemed to give way in the face of tragedy. After the quake sixty-one of the victims were flown to Israel, where they received seven months of medical care and rehabilitation — free. They all returned to their homeland in August 1989.

Why the outpouring of help? It came, the *New York Times* editorialized, for the plain and simple reason that the world knew that help was needed. People would have been equally generous to the people of China's quake-torn Yunnan Province eighteen years earlier if they had known a need existed. They would have helped the victims of earlier Soviet earthquakes as well. But human beings cannot even begin to try to solve problems unless they hear about those problems. That, above all, was the lesson of the great earthquake of 1988.

The Soviets seemed to have learned that lesson, and by 1990 glasnost had moved well beyond earthquake reporting. The difficulties of everyday Soviet life — shortages of consumer goods, agricultural failures, slow factory production — were for the first time acceptable topics of discussion. The government lifted some forms of censorship, too. For example, it stopped jamming radio broadcasts from other countries, including those from the U.S.-run Radio Liberty. Even military censorship was relaxed, at least to the degree that maps began showing towns, cities, bays, and rivers in their proper locations. Always before, strategic locations had been scrambled in order to fool possible enemy invaders. Soviet teachers were instructed to begin telling their students about some of the darker side of their country's history, including the fact that millions of citizens had been murdered and executed by order of dictator Joseph Stalin in a 1930s reign of terror. In another move that stunned most observers, the Soviet government admitted to an atrocity committed during World War II, the slaughter of 4,300 officers of the Polish army. Up until 1989 the Soviets had officially blamed the killings on Germany.

In Poland changes in the right to know were going on too, as they were in some of the other nations of Eastern Europe. Press restrictions were being eased, labor unions were gaining recognition, and limited free elections were taking place. In China the general loosening of prohibitions against freedom of speech and assembly helped lead up to the huge demonstrations of May 1989. The disappointment when those demonstrations ended in a massive crackdown and a new round of repression was felt around the world. People hoped that a similar reversion to past

ways would not happen in the Soviet Union and Eastern
Europe.

In other parts of the world besides China, the outlook
for democracy and the right to know seemed dismal. Much
of Latin America, from socialist Cuba and Nicaragua to
right-wing El Salvador and Paraguay, has a more or less
regulated press. Even in the more liberal nations of the
region freedom of the press is an iffy affair at best, with
restrictions eased one month only to be tightened again the
next. Halfway around the world in India, government-
owned radio and television have a monopoly on news and
information. The censorship imposed in South Africa under the emergency decree of 1986 was still in place four
years later, although there were signs that it might one day
be eased. The new white South African government that
came to power in 1989 was, at least, relaxing some of the
country's apartheid laws. Citizens of other African nations, including those with left-wing governments, also
live with censorship — and many resent the fact. "It is
high time the official, controlled, censored, muzzled or
partisan news gives way in Africa to news based on the
diversity of opinions and ideas," says a news agency director in the People's Republic of the Congo. "We need
to democratize the media in some of our countries."

Even in parts of Western Europe, some say, the media
could stand a bit of democratizing. *New York Times* columnist Anthony Lewis, who lived in England for years,
calls that nation's press "muzzled." Michael Kinsley of
The New Republic points out that English libel laws are

so strict that the press censors itself. "There is a growing movement in Britain for some kind of Bill of Rights," Kinsley wrote in 1989. "They certainly need one."

We in the United States have our Bill of Rights. We have our right to know. And, despite the ominous growth in government secrecy during the 1980s — a secrecy that goes beyond matters of national security to embrace basic science, industrial production, consumer affairs, environmental concerns, and a host of other areas — there are signs that the situation may improve in the decade ahead.

"The winds of change are blowing," President George Bush proclaimed in his January 1989 inauguration address. Within weeks, demonstrating a willingness to make himself part of the change, perhaps to step back in the direction of pre-Reagan-administration standards of openness in government, Bush announced his support for a bill designed to protect federal whistleblowers. The bill's intent was to keep agency directors from firing or demoting workers who call attention to unsafe or illegal conditions. The previous fall, shortly before leaving office, President Reagan had refused to sign a similar bill into law. In May 1989 the Nuclear Regulatory Commission (NRC), the federal agency that oversees the nuclear industry, reversed its earlier policy of allowing plant operators to pay potential whistleblowers to keep silent about violations of health and safety codes.

Whistleblowing may be one wave of the future. In 1988 it was Congress itself that blew the whistle about thirty-one years' worth of nuclear accidents at the gov-

ernment's weaponmaking facility at Savannah River,
South Carolina. Prospective whistleblowers may also be
encouraged to action by the fact that they can get legal
and financial support from an organization in Washington, D.C., the Government Accountability Project
(GAP). GAP solicits public contributions and regularly
updates members on its efforts to maintain high standards
in the nuclear industry, federal meat inspection programs,
building construction, and so forth.

Another hopeful sign for the right to know was that
after several months in office, President Bush seemed
prepared to hold more press conferences than his prede-
cessor. Whereas Reagan scheduled an average of only six
formal conferences a year, Bush, like earlier presidents,
made a habit of talking often with reporters, both formally and informally. Reagan, although he appeared willing to respond to reporters' questions, generally displayed
that willingness when he was about to board the presidential helicopter or was disembarking from it. Helicop-
ters are noisy machines, and Reagan, who was a little
deaf, reacted to shouted questions by cupping a hand
around his ear to indicate that he couldn't quite catch
what was being asked. Other presidents have seemed to
genuinely enjoy a bit of give-and-take with members of
the media.

Another possibility for change could be a return to
some earlier media rules. Congress might decide to rein-
state some form of fairness doctrine, for example. If that
happens, the doctrine will be a matter of legislation, and

no longer subject to manipulation by the executive branch. Reagan was adamantly opposed to a fairness law, but some analysts suspect that Bush may feel differently. Cable television, deregulated in the mid-1980s, might also find itself subject to new rules. By 1989 Congress was getting thousands of complaints about cutbacks in cable service combined with ever-increasing rate hikes.

Other hopeful signs come from media people themselves. Stung by criticism from politicians, the public, and such groups as AIM and FAIR, reporters, editors, and broadcasters are examining their own ethics as never before. In 1989 the *Christian Science Monitor* was calling on journalists who receive fees for speaking engagements or TV appearances to make public the size and sources of those fees. Top media stars can command up to $20,000 per appearance, the *Monitor* pointed out, enough to make it important for them to avoid even the hint of a conflict of interest.

A concern for professional ethics has led some news organizations to appoint ombudsmen. An ombudsman is someone within the organization who acts on behalf of the public, looking at news and information problems from a consumer's point of view and following up on complaints and criticisms. Other organizations have invited independent ethicists to study their operations and suggest ways to improve their news and information gathering and disseminating techniques. Print and broadcast journalists nationwide regularly convene to discuss reporting techniques, concern for profit margins, political bias in the media, and the like. Yet another goal for some in the media is to get more blacks, Hispanics, Asians, women, and others with non-white-male perspectives into newsrooms and broadcast studios.

Finally, media technology suggests hope for the future. The kind of reporting that came out of Beijing's Tiananmen Square during the people's protest there would have been almost unimaginable just a few years ago. The small camera-recorders called minicamcorders, as well as remote hookups and satellite transmissions were a large part of what made CNN's coverage of events outshine the CIA's. Of course, CNN was helped by the fact that China's government was doing very little censoring in May 1989.

Yet even when censorship is in place, technology can offer pathways around it. Israeli leaders kept U.S. television footage of intifada violence off the state-controlled airwaves in 1988, but they couldn't stop their people from getting a glimpse of that violence from other sources. Any Israeli with three dollars to spare could go to a theater to see weekly showings of American TV news reports from Gaza and the West Bank. The reports reached Israel via satellite and were collected by dish antennas there. At about the same time thousands of people in the Chinese-ruled nation of Tibet were staging riots and demanding independence. Chinese leaders assumed that if they kept journalists out of Tibet, they could keep word of the uprising from getting out as well. Not so. Tibetans and foreign tourists used hand-held video cameras to record the violence. Smuggled out to the West, the video depictions helped create headlines.

Computers could be another vital element in future information sharing. As science journalist Ivars Peterson reported in 1988, "The United States already has more than 100 computer networks, linking government laboratories, Defense Department operations, groups of universities, and researchers within specialized fields . . . Many large companies operate private networks carrying data to and from facilities all over the world." Right now, says computer expert Robert E. Kahn, such systems are in their infancy. He compares getting information from them to traveling coast to coast by automobile in 1900. Ninety years ago there were no road maps or signs, no service stations, no interconnected federal highways. Drivers had to search out their own routes and carry their own gasoline, tools, and spare parts. "That's very close to what computing is like today," Kahn says, but he predicts that this will change, and soon. One indication that he is right: in April 1989 the American Telephone & Telegraph Company (AT&T) applied for permission to create and transmit computerized information services using its long-distance lines.

Will new services like these and the other technologies that are bound to come along enhance our right to know? Or will they be restricted by the type of rules so popular in the 1980s? Only we the people — citizens of a democracy that has grown and flourished along with the public right to know — can provide the answers.

For Further Reading

Ayars, James. *We Hold These Truths, From Magna Carta to the Bill of Rights*. New York: Viking Press, 1977.

Carter, Joseph. *Freedom to Know, A Background Book*. New York: Parents' Magazine Press, 1974.

Hentoff, Nat. *The First Freedom: The Tumultuous History of Free Speech in America*. New York: Delacorte, 1980.

Rogers, Donald J. *Press vs. Government: Constitutional Issues*. New York: Messner, 1987.

Bibliography

Chapter 1

Kristof, Nicholas D. "Chinese Disclose That Quake in 1970 Killed about 10,000." *New York Times,* Nov. 19, 1988.

————. "What's the Law in China? It's No Secret (Finally)." *New York Times,* Nov. 20, 1988.

Noble, Kenneth B. "After Forty Years, the Silence is Broken on a Troubled Nuclear Arms Industry." *New York Times,* Oct. 10, 1988.

Oboler, Eli M. *To Free the Mind: Libraries, Technology, and Intellectual Freedom.* Littleton, Colo.: Libraries Unlimited, 1983.

Chapters 2–3

Downs, Robert B., and Ralph E. McCoy, eds. *The First Freedom Today.* Chicago: American Library Association, 1984.

Geller, Evelyn. *Forbidden Books in American Public Libraries, 1876–1939.* Westport, Conn.: Greenwood Press, 1984.

Pell, Eve. *The Big Chill.* Boston: Beacon Press, 1984.

Riley, Tom, and Harold C. Relyea, eds. *Freedom of Information Trends in the Information Age.* London: Frank Cass and Company, 1983.

Wiggins, James Russell. *Freedom or Secrecy.* New York: Oxford University Press, 1956.

Chapter 4

Blau, Eleanor. "CNN Basks in Reaction to Its Beijing Coverage." *New York Times,* May 25, 1989.

Boyer, Peter J. "Once an Embattled Show, 'Newshour' Gains Friends." *New York Times,* Dec. 17, 1989.

Dowd, Maureen. "Where Bush Turns for the Latest." *New York Times,* Aug. 11, 1989.

Gerard, Jeremy. "Walter Cronkite: Speaking His Mind Instead of Just News." *New York Times,* Jan. 8, 1989.

Greenwald, John. "Tune In, Turn On, Sort Out." *Time,* May 29, 1989.

Jamieson, Kathleen Hall. "Lies Televised." *National Voter,* Apr./ May 1989.

Kagan, Daniel. "Viable Alternatives to the Big Press." *Insight,* Jan. 23, 1989.

Vidal, Gore. "Cue the Green God, Ted." *Nation,* Aug. 7/14, 1989.

Zoglin, Richard. "Bugle Boys of the Airwaves." *Time,* May 15, 1989.

Chapter 5

Altman, Lawrence K. "Medical Guardians." *New York Times,* Jan. 28, 1988.

Barron, Jerome A. *Freedom of the Press for Whom?* Bloomington, Ind.: Indiana University Press, 1973.

Cowan, Robert C. "Report on Aspirin: Public Knowledge vs. Private Profits." *Christian Science Monitor,* Feb. 2, 1988.

Friendly, Fred W. "On Television: News, Lies and Videotape." *New York Times,* Aug. 6, 1989.

Gerard, Jeremy. "PBS and Two of Its Affiliates Dispute Film on Palestinians." *New York Times,* May 2, 1989.

Goodman, Walter. "Commercial TV Gets Commercial Threats." *New York Times,* Apr. 24, 1989.

Jones, Alex S. "For New Magazines, Growing Identity Crisis." *New York Times,* June 29, 1988.

Lohr, Steve. "Media Mergers: An Urge to Get Bigger and More Global." *New York Times,* Mar. 19, 1989.

McFadden, Robert D. "Suspect in Five Killings in 1971 Caught with Aid of TV Show." *New York Times,* June 2, 1989.

O'Connor, John J. "The Mystery of the Korean Airliner." *New York Times,* Nov. 28, 1988.

Rosenbaum, David E. "On TV, Col. North Meets Reality He Never Faced." *New York Times,* Apr. 28, 1989.

Zuckerman, Laurence. "Who's Running the Newsroom?" *Time,* Nov. 28, 1988.

Chapter 6

"Eyeless in Gaza and the West Bank." *New York Times,* Apr. 5, 1988.

Kollek, Teddy. "Israel and the Palestinian Uprising — Is TV Making It Worse?" *TV Guide,* Oct. 29, 1988.

Chapter 7

Bradley, Barbara. "Hostage Takers in U.S. Aping Foreign Terrorists." *Christian Science Monitor,* Feb. 4, 1988.

"Brotherly Media." *Nation,* June 12, 1989.

"Denying the News." *Christian Science Monitor,* Mar. 10, 1988.

Goodman, Walter. "News Programs and Social Problems." *New York Times,* July 6, 1988.

"Police Say ABC Made Early Drug Raid Necessary." *New York Times,* Apr. 12, 1988.

Rabin, Roni C. "Israeli TV's Editing Brings Harsh Questions." *New York Times,* Mar. 3, 1988.

Rosenthal, A. M. "This Censored World." *New York Times,* Apr. 26, 1988.

Sullivan, Cheryl, and Scott Armstrong. "Exit Polls That Chill Western Elections." *Christian Science Monitor,* Nov. 8, 1988.

Chapter 8

Altman, Lawrence K. "Fitness for Office." *New York Times,* Aug. 5, 1988.

Apple, R. W. "Changing Morality: Press and Politics." *New York Times,* May 6, 1987.

Foster, Catherine. "Lawyers Assail Rise in Court Secrecy." *Christian Science Monitor,* Aug. 4, 1989.

Herbers, John. "On Private Transgressions and Holding the Public Trust." *New York Times,* Mar. 3, 1985.

Hinds, Michael deCourcy. "Personal but Not Confidential: A New Debate over Privacy." *New York Times,* Feb. 27, 1988.

Jacobs, Joanne. "Lying Can't Be Justified." *San Jose Mercury News,* Aug. 14, 1989.

Jones, Alex S. "Less Is Best, Press Says, in Naming Rape Victims." *New York Times,* June 22, 1989.

Kenney, Charles. "The Prosecutorial Press." *Boston Globe,* Apr. 17, 1988.

McFadden, Robert D. "Court Challenges Scholars' Right to Quote from Private Documents." *New York Times,* Apr. 28, 1989.

Montgomery, Peter. "Public Figures/Private Lives." *Common Cause,* Sept.-Oct. 1988.

Scardino, Albert. "Appeals Court Turns Down Suit against Author." *New York Times,* Aug. 5, 1989.

Taylor, Stuart, Jr. "Court, 8–0, Refuses to Curb Criticism of Public Figures." *New York Times,* Feb. 25, 1988.

Zuckerman, Laurence. "Knocking on Death's Door." *Time,* Feb. 27, 1989.

————. "Sticky Issues in Gumshoe Journalism." *Time,* Aug. 8, 1988.

Chapter 9

Burgower, Barbara. "A Living Nightmare." *Ladies' Home Journal,* Mar. 1989.

Demac, Donna A. *Liberty Denied: The Current Rise of Censorship in America.* New York: PEN American Center, 1988.

Halloran, Richard. "Stealth Sheds Secrets, but Its Cost Stays Hidden." *New York Times,* Dec. 14, 1988.

Johnston, David. "Documents Disclose F.B.I. Investigations of Some Librarians." *New York Times,* Nov. 7, 1989.

Kahler, Kathryn. "The FBI's Library Caper." *Boston Globe,* Nov. 27, 1988.

Pell, Eve. "The Backbone of Hidden Government." *Nation,* June 19, 1989.

————. *The Big Chill.* Boston: Beacon Press, 1984.

Schneider, Keith. "Accidents at a U.S. Nuclear Plant Were Kept Secret up to 31 Years." *New York Times,* Oct. 1, 1988.

Shattuck, John, and Muriel Morisey Spence. "The Dangers of Information Control." *Technology Review,* April 1988.

Sullivan, Joseph F. "Student Wants F.B.I. File Purged." *New York Times,* Nov. 12, 1989.

Varlejs, Jana, ed. *Freedom of Information and Youth.* Jefferson, N.C.: McFarland & Company, 1986.

Chapter 10

Bernstein, Richard. "At Beijing Ministry of Truth, History Is Quickly Rewritten." *New York Times,* June 12, 1989.

Jones, Alex S. "True or False, and Who Says?" *New York Times,* Oct. 13, 1986.

Kamm, Henry. "Was Austere Envoy a Spy? In Austria, It's 'Unthinkable.' " *New York Times,* Aug. 2, 1989.

Shabecoff, Philip. "Scientist Says Budget Office Altered His Testimony." *New York Times,* May 8, 1989.

Sidey, Hugh. "A Busy Thursday." *Time,* May 22, 1989.

Smolowe, Jill. "Deng's Big Lie." *Time,* June 26, 1989.

Taylor, Stuart, Jr. "Court Ruling on Leaks Could Make It a Crime to Talk to the Press." *New York Times,* Apr. 10, 1988.

Van Voorst, Bruce. "The Stealth Takes Wing." *Time,* July 31, 1989.

Wald, Matthew L. "Retribution Seen in Atom Industry." *New York Times,* Aug. 6, 1989.

WuDunn, Sheryl. "Giving the Official Spin: Six Scenes on Chinese TV." *New York Times,* June 15, 1989.

Chapter 11

Brinkley, Joel. "Israel Tends to Quake Victims and Soviet Ties." *New York Times,* Aug. 16, 1989.

Jones, Alex S. "Black Journalists Seeking New Gains in the Newsroom." *New York Times,* Aug. 17, 1989.

————. "Of Hiring Minorities and Newsroom Ethics." *New York Times,* Apr. 15, 1989.

Peterson, Ivars. "Highways for Information." *Science News,* June 18, 1988.

Rowe, Jonathan. "Media Watchdog Group Sees Pro-Establishment Bias in News Reporting." *Christian Science Monitor,* Mar. 7, 1989.

Sims, Calvin. "AT&T Is Proposing to Offer Electronic Publishing Service." *New York Times,* Apr. 22, 1989.

Index